KILLER SPECIES

ultimate attack

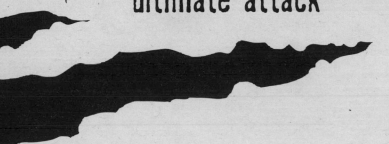

KILLER SPECIES
ultimate attack

Michael P. Spradlin

SCHOLASTIC INC.

ISBN 978-0-545-50678-6

Copyright © 2014 by Michael P. Spradlin
Interior art by Jeff Weigel

12 11 10 9 8 7 6 5 4 3 2 1   14 15 16 17 18 19/0

Printed in the U.S.A.   40
First printing, July 2014

The display type was set in Badhouse Light.
The text type was set in Apollo MT.
Book design by Nina Goffi

To the Mackey family.
Bruce, Tammy, Alex, Jordan, and Nathan.
You live in Florida. Don't look out the window.
I'm just saying.

1

IT WAS STILL SO HARD FOR HIM TO ACCEPT.

Up until this moment, almost everything had gone wrong. Unexpected forces were aligned against him. Variables not considered in his equations and simulations somehow appeared with regularity. There was no doubt about it: Dr. Catalyst's plan to restore the Florida ecosystem was falling apart before his eyes.

Everything that could go wrong did. One by one, his Pterogators were being gathered up in the Everglades. While their introduction dramatically reduced the snake population, they had not eradicated the pythons and boa constrictors as he had hoped. His Muraecudas put a severe dent in the number of lionfish on the coastal reefs. But apparently they'd migrated to other waters, or had perhaps fallen victim to sharks or bigger predators. None had been sighted in weeks, and the lionfish were returning.

And the media was reporting that his Blood Jackets, which he considered his crowning achievement, were dying off. Scores of them had been found dead all over Florida City and the surrounding countryside. He hadn't even been able to recover the body of the inept Dr. Newton from the swamp. Surely the man was dead, but it was a loose end, and Dr. Catalyst did not like loose ends.

It felt as if he was teetering on the brink of total failure. Early on in his campaign, he had issued a manifesto. Sent to hundreds of media outlets and posted online, it called for like-minded individuals to join his efforts. It was his hope to start a movement, to rally others to his side. It had utterly failed. No one had offered to join him. A few fringe environmental groups had "endorsed" his efforts, but Dr. Catalyst had envisioned throngs of people — hundreds, if not thousands — flocking to his cause. They never materialized. The media called him a crackpot and a danger to society. How preposterous.

He was a visionary.

Still, despite his genius, his efforts had not had the desired effects. And there was one reason. In his mind, his creatures would be healing the fragile Florida ecosystem right now if not for the harassment and interference of a particular individual.

Emmet Doyle.

When the Doyle brat showed up — that was when his plans had gone awry. Someone not even old enough to shave was dashing his hopes and dreams for a naturally restored Florida Everglades. Interfering. Agitating. Forcing him to divert his precious time and resources from his mission. And now he was left with no other choice but to remove this obstacle. No matter the cost.

Prior to releasing his creatures, Dr. Catalyst had purchased over two dozen vehicles. It had been comically simple for someone of his brilliance to hack into the Florida Department of Motor Vehicles registration database and create false registrations and titles of ownership for each vehicle.

One of them, a dark brown panel van, was parked at the curb a few hundred yards down the street from the Doyle home. The windows on the rear door were tinted, allowing no one to see inside. A few ventilation slots were cut into the vehicle to allow air to circulate. The name of a famous national delivery service company had been painted on the side. The van's license plate and registration would easily pass muster if he were to meet a police officer. Provided they did not ask him to open the rear doors. No one must view his cargo.

That would be a problem.

As if to illustrate his point, the van jerked on its suspension and a strange growling, laughing roar came from the van's cargo bay. His newest creation was keen to steal into the night. A low growl sounded through the rear wall of the van, and the vehicle bounced again as the creature threw itself against its cage. It was eager to be set free. To hunt.

But patience was required.

At his campaign's start, Dr. Catalyst had placed video and audio recording devices at National Park Service headquarters. It allowed him to keep tabs on the comings and goings of Dr. Geaux and Dr. Doyle, and on their efforts to thwart him. Somehow they had discovered he was monitoring them and staged a futile attempt to capture him by feeding him false information. He had easily seen through their feeble deception. However, they had removed his surveillance equipment. Now he no longer had inside information on the movements of his enemies.

Dr. Catalyst paused mid-thought. He could hear muffled growls and groans from the animal in back. The van shook again as the creature launched itself repeatedly at the side of its cage. He had not fed it yet today, deciding that hunger would hone its hunting instincts.

Finally the animal quieted. Dr. Catalyst resumed watching the street.

The loss of his equipment forced him to resort to actual physical observation. He couldn't trust replacing the bugs at the park offices or on Doyle's and Geaux's vehicles. They were now regularly checked for listening devices. So he did it the old-fashioned way. Trailing them around town. Spying on them whenever he could do so unobserved, until he had enough data on their routine behavior for his next grand demonstration.

It took precious time away from his work, but eliminating Emmet Doyle would also remove Dr. Doyle and Dr. Geaux from the equation. Then his mission could continue.

His fleet of vehicles had come in handy as he followed Emmet and his father at various times during the day and night. Tonight was Thursday. On Thursdays, Emmet and his father joined Dr. Geaux and Calvin at Pompano's Pizzeria and did not return until after 9 P.M.

Dr. Catalyst looked at his watch. 9:10 P.M. They would be arriving any moment. As if on cue, he saw their pickup truck in his driver's-side mirror, turning onto the street. He leaned down in the seat as their truck passed by, making sure they didn't spot him. A lone man sitting in a van at night might be remembered. An empty vehicle would draw little attention. The truck passed by and continued down the street until it turned into their driveway. He sat up, watching as Emmet and his dad exited the pickup and entered their home.

On the seat next to him sat a pistol loaded with an extremely powerful tranquilizer dart. In the unlikely event that the creature in back decided to turn on him, he would need it. Next to it was a cattle prod. Dr. Catalyst was not cruel to animals, nor was he particularly worried it might attack him. It had been engineered and trained to seek out only one prey.

Still, Dr. Catalyst muttered his mantra.

"No chances."

Scanning the street, he confirmed that no one was around. He grabbed the tranquilizer gun and cattle prod, then opened the door. Quietly, he stole toward the rear of the van. Dr. Catalyst holstered the pistol and put his free hand on the door handle. Flicking the switch on the cattle prod, he heard a whirring hum as the device charged.

Dr. Catalyst took a deep breath. Once the rear door was opened, a system of cables and pulleys attached to the cage gate would raise it, and his creature would bound from the van.

And it would hunt.

It growled again, and the van shook once more. It was almost as if the creature could sense that it was about to be set free. And it was impatient. Dr. Catalyst pushed a button on a small device attached to his wristband. It sent a signal to a collar the creature wore, delivering a mild electric shock to the beast. From within the bowels of the van, Dr. Catalyst heard a cackling laugh from the animal. The "laughing" sound signified submission to a superior.

What waited inside the pen was his latest hybrid. A singular creation. It was not made to counter an invasive species. It was not born in his lab to prevent the destruction of the Everglades. This beast had one purpose and one purpose only.

To find, follow, and kill Emmet Doyle.

Dr. Catalyst opened the door and heard the squeak of cables and pulleys raising the gate to the metal cage. He stepped behind the van door, peeking around to view the magnificent animal emerging from the dark interior. It strode to the edge of the cargo bay and stood in the open rear doorway. It sniffed the night air, then raised its head and howled its odd and terrifying cry. It was half the laugh of a hyena, and the other half the growl of the Florida panther.

It was a terrifying monster. It had the long tail and strong, thickly muscled rear legs of the panther. The front legs, spotted coloring, and head were all hyena.

Except for the jaws.

The jaws and fangs were a wicked combination of each species. Two rows of razor-sharp teeth emerged from its mouth. It looked as if hunting knives were somehow growing from each jaw.

For a moment, Dr. Catalyst worried the creature would not leave. It sat on the edge of the van, surveying the night. Ever since his Pterogators were first released, Emmet Doyle had interfered at every turn. After Emmet rescued his father in the swamp, Dr. Catalyst began to prepare for this eventuality. As he nursed his wounds and cursed his fate, he had understood the boy and his father would continue to be a problem. And they had thwarted him again and again. The only solution to the obstacle was to eliminate it. So he created what now stood there, still and silent. He savored the moment.

Each stage of his experiments produced vast improvements in his gene splicing, recombinant DNA, and accelerated growth methods. Until the Blood Jackets, which appeared to be dying out. He suspected the cause was that the two species used to create them were too divergent.

But hyenas were a close relative of the feline family — although they resembled dogs, and most people assumed they were canines. Dr. Catalyst was sure this combination of species would be his greatest achievement yet. It had to be. There was too much at stake. Once he had created a predator that could identify, stalk, and eliminate a single target, there would be no limits on the environmental damage he could reverse. With this technique perfected, he could generate an entire species that would cull other invasive species all over the world.

The genes of the panther would create a stalking predator that would fixate on its prey. The hyena genes forged a relentless and fearless hunter. Hyenas excelled at hunting, despite their reputation as scavengers. And they were ferocious in their own right, often driving off much bigger leopards and lionesses from their kills. The look of the animal alone would send terror coursing through Emmet Doyle. Dr. Catalyst's face twisted into a snarl. How he wished he could be there the first time the obnoxious little brat encountered the animal. To see the fear and terror in his eyes would be such a thrill. Instead, he would have to settle for letting his surrogate enjoy the final victory.

The great beast sniffed the air again, and Dr. Catalyst pushed the button on the cattle prod, hearing a crackle of electricity as it discharged. He hoped it would not require any convincing to leave. But he would be ready if it did.

But he needn't have worried. Using powerful hind legs, it leapt from the van and landed deftly on the blacktop. Without looking back, it trotted away. For a brief moment Dr. Catalyst wondered if he would ever see it again. There was a tracking device inserted in the skin beneath its neck, but who knew how long the power would last?

The creature stopped in the middle of the street and inhaled the night air. It paused, shaking its head back and forth, as if trying to focus. Then it caught the scent it desired and loped away into the darkness.

Heading directly for the Doyle home.

2

SECRETS.

Emmet knew that everyone had them. Some kept them. Others didn't. There were some kinds of people who, the minute you told them your secret, they blabbed it to everyone. In some cases, it wasn't malicious. Emmet's mother had always told him there are some people who just can't help being blabbermouths. He laughed at the memory. That was the exact word his mother used. *Blabbermouths*. He missed his mom. She had a way of cutting through everything and getting right to the crux of the matter. Like when people were blabbermouths.

Sometimes people shared your secret on purpose. Maybe to get you into trouble. Or to watch you squirm, when you knew people were talking about you behind your back.

There were those, however, who would never reveal a secret. You could trust them with the deepest, darkest thing you could possibly imagine. They would never say a word to anyone. It just wasn't in them.

Emmet found that Calvin Geaux was like that. Calvin kept your secrets. (As long as the secret didn't involve something illegal, dangerous to yourself or others, or that might cause unnecessary dirt to get on his boat or something.)

But just as he would keep your secrets, he also kept his own.

You could plead with him, cajole him, threaten him, and it didn't matter. Emmet was pretty sure Calvin could survive having a truckload of bricks dumped on him, and he still wouldn't give up a secret. You could force Calvin to go to the latest concert of the most current, hottest boy band, surrounded by ten thousand screaming twelve-year-old girls, make him stay through the entire thing — twice — and he still wouldn't tell.

It was really starting to tick Emmet off.

The reason it made him so angry is that Calvin knew the biggest secret of all. Not the secret to faster-than-light travel or who invented liquid soap. He knew the one true thing Emmet wanted to know more than anything else.

The real identity of Dr. Catalyst.

A few weeks ago, Calvin disappeared into the swamp. He wasn't gone very long — less than twenty-four hours. But long enough for everyone to know he was missing. Dr. Geaux organized a search, but Calvin returned from his quest just in time to save Emmet, Riley, and Raeburn. The three of them were about to be overrun by Blood Jackets and Pterogators after their airboat broke down.

As they raced away from the danger, Calvin had told Emmet that he knew who Dr. Catalyst really was. His clandestine trip deep into the swamp to discover the identity of the crazed environmentalist was successful. Calvin believed he had uncovered the madman's identity.

But that was then and this was now.

And Calvin wasn't talking.

When the kids got back, Dr. Geaux was both relieved and furious with Calvin for running off. (And with Emmet, Riley, and Raeburn for going after him.) All Calvin would say about why he had disappeared was "I had something I had to do," so she grounded him for six weeks. She also took away the keys to his airboat so if he ran off again he would need to travel by other means.

Emmet didn't think that grounding Calvin did any good. It appeared as if he actually enjoyed it. He swept out the tree house and built some shelves for it. His room was even more spotless. One day he was so bored he organized their entire garage. Dr. Geaux was completely exasperated. Although even she had to admit the garage was remarkably clean. Being grounded also offered Calvin ample opportunities to sit quietly without moving for hours at a time. Something he seemed to enjoy a great deal. On the discipline-effectiveness scale it didn't appear to have much impact. Calvin still wasn't talking.

Dr. Geaux kept telling Calvin all he had to do was "speak up" and "explain himself" and his punishment would end. Of course, this would never happen. Emmet knew that Calvin wasn't going to say anything until he was good and ready.

And it was getting in the way of their friendship.

Emmet was in a mood all day. The silence at the pizza place was thicker than the deep-dish pepperoni pie they'd ordered.

"Everything okay between you and Calvin, son?" Emmet's dad asked as they pulled into the driveway.

"Yeah. Fine."

"Didn't sound fine. Didn't sound fine at all at dinner. You were both as quiet as stones. Calvin doesn't talk much on a good day, but you're usually up for some enjoyable conversation."

Emmet sighed. "I don't know. I guess I'm just tired."

His dad didn't press it, which Emmet appreciated.

Even though Calvin was still technically grounded, Dr. Geaux let him come along for their pizza outing every Thursday. Emmet thought it was more because she liked spending time with his dad. Calvin's secret-keeping shouldn't interfere with their blossoming relationship.

Just because Emmet was a kid didn't mean he didn't get stuff. His dad and Dr. Geaux liked each other. Whatever. He had more important things to worry about.

Apollo was barking madly when they walked up the front steps. This was not unusual. He always howled, yipped, and squeaked whenever they returned from anywhere and he had not been allowed to go along — something he considered a federal crime.

There were four stages of greeting whenever they returned.

First, he would be scratching at the door as it was opened and would jump on Emmet or his dad as they stepped through, barking and yapping, then rolling over on his back for a belly rub as if they'd left him alone for weeks. The fact that they'd been gone less than ninety minutes was lost on him.

Second, he would spring to his feet and begin sniffing their shoes and legs, and then stand on his hind legs and smell their pockets. He was checking to see if they had encountered anything from the animal kingdom that had left its scent on them. Or if they had, by any chance, brought home anything edible. And Apollo had a wide range of things he considered edible.

The third stage would be indignation. Emmet would say, "Hi, buddy!" and reach down to scratch his ears. Apollo would race away a few feet, just out of reach. This was supposed to be Emmet's punishment for abandoning him. It usually lasted all of ten seconds, until Apollo gave in, raced forward, and entered the fourth stage, which was repeating the entire process all over again.

But this time when Emmet and his dad entered the house, Apollo didn't engage in his regular routine. He barked in happiness, but in the middle of the first belly rub, sprang to his feet and raced to the back door. He lifted his head and howled. His howl was high-pitched and sounded funny. It was usually reserved for when he spotted a jogger on the street, or the mailman delivered the mail, or an unauthorized leaf had the gall to blow across the front yard.

"What's gotten into him?" asked Emmet's dad as they followed him into the kitchen.

"Beats me," Emmet said. He looked at Apollo's water dish. It had been full when they left, but was more than half empty now.

"Maybe he really has to go," he said.

Emmet's backyard was securely fenced in to keep alligators out. They lived in Florida, after all, a place where you had to consider the possibility that a two-hundred-million-year-old species of killing machine might casually stroll into your backyard if it was left unfenced. Especially if you had pets. People who didn't live there did not have to think about this. Emmet himself still wasn't used to it.

The yard had a small stone patio and three cypress trees. Dr. Catalyst had kidnapped Apollo from it not too long ago. Since that happened, they had motion-sensor lights mounted on the wall on either side of the door. Anytime Apollo went outside for his nightly ritual, either Emmet or his dad made sure to watch over him.

Apollo was acting really weird. He was anxious to get outside, running back and forth between Emmet and the door. Emmet nearly tripped over him several times on the way. As he pulled it open the first few inches, with Apollo desperately trying to squirm his way through the tiniest opening, it suddenly registered that the yard lights were shining brightly. They shouldn't have been, unless something in the back-yard . . . something moving around . . . had turned them on.

Emmet had his hand on the doorknob. Apollo was still howling. His dad had stopped paying attention and was sorting through the mail. The door was open about a foot wide when something big and brown and furry catapulted into it so hard it knocked him to the ground.

"Emmet!" He heard his dad shout. Or at least he thought it was his dad. He was a little stunned, what with the falling to the ground and banging his head on the floor. Slowly, Emmet raised his head up to see Apollo crouched with his back low to the ground, his teeth bared, and the fur on his back standing almost straight up.

The screen door had saved them. Whatever had launched itself at Emmet and Apollo was now tangled up in the screen. All Emmet could see was a head peeking through the open space where the door had gotten lodged against his feet.

A terrifying head. Or more accurately, giant, sharp teeth that happened to be attached to a head. It had a furry face and a snout and muzzle kind of like a dog. And it alternated between a mewling growl like a cat and a weird laughing sound.

But it was mad and hungry and trying to get inside.

"Apollo! Off! Off!" Emmet heard his dad shout. That was Apollo's command to stop and stand down. But he was beyond that. Most of the time he obeyed. But this was different. His personal space was about to be invaded by a . . . giant, toothy . . . thing. He leapt at the head and was about to land right inside its mouth when Emmet found the strength to reach up and snatch his hind leg, pulling him backward. He was twenty-five pounds of fury.

Emmet kicked hard at the door with his foot and heard the creature snarl in anger. Then his dad flew into his field of vision, throwing his shoulder hard into the door. Whatever was trying to get in yowled in pain, but did not retreat.

"Push!" Emmet shouted. He lifted both feet and jammed them firmly against the door. Luckily it was made of thick, sturdy cypress planks, because whatever this thing was, it was clearly ferocious.

Emmet pushed with his legs as hard as he could, but this was one strong animal. For a second Emmet swore it locked its eyes on his. It howled that weird combination of barking and growling sounds. It was a sound like a cat and dog mixed in a blender. He felt like it stared at him forever, and in that gaze Emmet became truly afraid. The beast's eyes were cunning. It knew him, and it wanted nothing more than to kill him. When it snarled, its face kind of changed. One moment it looked like some kind of wild cat, and another like a hyena. How could that be?

"Push, Emmet!" his ever-helpful dad yelled.

"I am!" Emmet shouted. He was also holding a very angry little schnoodle by the hind leg, who was doing everything in his power to get loose and jump into the fight.

Even with its neck stuck in the door, the creature refused to withdraw.

"Hang on!" Emmet's dad yelled. He turned his back to the door and shoved as hard as he could. With his left hand his dad reached over toward the corner where they kept a broom. It was just out of his reach.

"What are you doing?" Emmet yelled at him. His legs were starting to shake. He was losing strength. The creature kept wiggling and squirming, hammering its body against the door, desperate to get in.

Emmet's dad must have managed to get ahold on the broom, because in the next moment Emmet heard a whistling sound and a loud crack as the broom handle connected with the creature's snout. It howled in rage. The broomstick hit it again and this time it jerked back and they were able to jam the door shut. Emmet's dad flipped the lock. The animal was furious, throwing its body at the door over and over, scratching and clawing while Apollo answered each attack with a bark and growl of his own, daring the monster to come inside and face schnoodle justice. Then, eventually, it was silent.

His dad raced to the front door and locked it, then shut the doors to all of the bedrooms, in case it crashed through one of their windows. Emmet wasn't sure the interior doors would hold it. No, with his luck, it had opposable thumbs and could turn doorknobs.

His dad came back to the kitchen and fell to his knees beside him, cradling Emmet's head in his lap.

"Are you okay?" he asked.

"Yeah. I think so," Emmet said.

His head was spinning and his legs were throbbing. Apollo stopped barking and turned his attention to licking Emmet's face, as if he was trying to revive him. His dad used his cell phone to call 9-1-1. His voice sounded like it was a million miles away.

As Emmet lay there staring up at the ceiling, he could only think of one thing.

How much he hated their backyard.

3

DR. CATALYST COULD HARDLY CONTAIN HIS GLEE. AS soon as the creature left the van he closed the rear doors and drove away from the neighborhood. Steering into a nearby shopping center parking lot, he pulled up a screen showing the tracker for his hybrid on his tablet. The program he used showed a small red dot moving along a map of the surrounding area. The red dot was the animal's transmitter location.

The GPS program was accurate to twenty-five feet. Swiping the screen, he zoomed in on the locator. He almost clapped his hands when he saw it blinking in the backyard of the Doyle home. It was already there. The creature could find and follow a scent better than he could have imagined.

It had taken some doing to train it to focus on Emmet Doyle. In order to provide the animal with the boy's unique aroma, he returned to Tasker Middle School a few days after the Blood Jacket incident. The school had remained closed for several days after the attack. Late at night he sneaked passed the very lax security post and broke inside. Checking records in the school office, he found Emmet's locker number and combination. There he found a jacket, a pair of tennis shoes, and a treasure trove of other materials he would need for his experiment.

Dr. Catalyst had purchased a four-hundred-acre farm to train the creature. The farm had originally been intended for use as an ostrich ranch and was equipped with a suitable barn and sufficiently high fences to prevent the creature's escape. It was well out of the metropolitan area, at the end of a long dirt road with no neighbors close by.

It was more than enough space to train the fast-growing hybrid. Dr. Catalyst used the odors embedded in Emmet's clothing to teach the hybrid to focus on that smell alone. Whenever it followed the scent to an article of Emmet's clothing, it was rewarded with a specially prepared, uniquely rich mixture of food. Soon the creature grew to crave the special food it earned. When it followed the wrong scent, it received nothing. After a few weeks, the beast would bypass everything from raw meat to other types of prey placed in its path to get to its target.

Like his Pterogators, Dr. Catalyst had trained it to respond to a homing beacon. When he was in an appropriate place he would activate the beacon. There was no sense in risking the animal being destroyed or captured before it completed its mission.

Now it was in the Doyles' backyard. Dr. Catalyst wished he were able to attach a video camera to the animal somehow. He knew from kidnapping the Doyles' stupid, yapping, tablet-stealing, leg-biting dog that Emmet let it out into the backyard every night before going to sleep. Since he had captured the mutt, they installed some primitive security measures — motion-sensor lights and such — but they would not deter the monster he created. It would be the last door Emmet ever opened.

Dr. Catalyst watched the blinking light for a while. It remained in the backyard. A few minutes later it began moving. It was now trailing along the canal that ran behind the house. The Doyles' home sat on a dead-end street and he would need to be careful. But he could not resist driving by and at least attempting to get a glimpse of the carnage.

There was a police scanner installed in the van. He flipped it on. Sure enough, emergency vehicles were on the way to the Doyle address, including an ambulance. He started the engine and pulled out of the lot. Rolling down the driver's-side window, he could hear the sirens approaching.

It was a very good night. A very good night indeed.

Dr. Catalyst sighed. His moment of victory was not as satisfying as he thought it would be. He thought he would feel triumphant, but instead he felt . . . confused.

For so long, he tried using his wealth and influence to focus attention on the plight of the Everglades and the entire South Florida ecosystem. But years of dealing with lobbyists, politicians, and bureaucrats had gotten him exactly nowhere.

It was the inaction of others that had forced him to take his brilliant scientific mind and put it to work on a solution. He'd concluded that introducing his own genetically altered creatures was the only option. Perhaps if someone — anyone — had listened to him, things might have gone differently. Now there was no turning back.

In the beginning, he had only meant to scare off Emmet and Calvin. To frighten them enough so they would stop interfering in his plans. But Dr. Geaux refused to back off. It was her fault he had to kidnap the lad's father, to show everyone how serious he was.

He was never going to harm the man. But the Doyle brat had taken things personally and caused everything to escalate.

As he drove, he began to feel better. Whatever fate had befallen that horrid child, he had brought it upon himself. Dr. Catalyst was not to blame.

The fault lay entirely with Emmet Doyle.

4

THE LIGHT WAS REALLY BRIGHT IN EMMET'S EYES. A doctor whose name Emmet had already forgotten was holding one of those tiny flashlights about an inch from his eyeball. The doctor asked Emmet to follow his finger back and forth without moving his head. Emmet was still hyped up from nearly being eaten by a gigantic, laughing, saber-toothed whatchamacallit. All the little tests were annoying.

"I don't see any signs of a concussion, but there's a nasty bump on the back of his head. I'd like to keep him overnight for observation," Dr. What's-His-Name told Emmet's dad.

"Okay," Dr. Doyle answered tiredly.

"But, Dad! I don't want to stay in the stu —" His dad interrupted him by holding his hand up. Dr. Doyle was generally likeable and easygoing about most things. But when he was wearing his parent pants, he was not open to discussing anything. This was one of those times. When his dad held the hand up while Emmet was complaining, whining, or talking, the discussion was over.

"You're staying. And I'm staying with you," he said.

"I'm afraid that's not allowed," the doctor said. He was busy writing something in a chart hanging from Emmet's bed. He wasn't paying attention as Dr. Doyle strolled up to him, close enough to invade his personal space.

"Doctor," he said quietly. "Tonight something tried to kill my son and me. It almost succeeded. If you think you're getting me out of this room tonight, you're going to need a lot more muscle."

Dr. Geaux was standing off to the side with Calvin. They had met Emmet and his dad at the hospital. Dr. Geaux looked weary and worried. Calvin's eyes were a little more wide open than usual. In Calvin, this meant he was alarmed and concerned. Otherwise he just seemed like regular Calvin, sitting in a chair not saying much.

"Ben," Dr. Geaux started. "I can have a couple officers —"

Dr. Doyle gave Dr. Geaux the hand.

"No, Rosalita," he said. Probably more sternly than he meant to, Emmet thought. "Thank you. If you want officers outside in the hall, fine. But I'm not leaving my son's side."

"That violates hospital policy. I'm afraid for the patient's sake —" the doctor started speaking again, but Dr. Doyle stepped closer, his nose now inches from the doctor's.

"Maybe I didn't make myself clear: I'm not leaving."

Truthfully, Emmet's dad was kind of surprising him. This was a side of him he'd never seen before. Benton Doyle was not what anyone would call a tough guy. But he was an avid outdoorsman, really smart, and he loved Emmet. In Montana, he'd hiked all over the mountains and sometimes led search-and-rescue teams to find lost and stranded hikers. He kept himself in shape, and tonight the doctor saw something in Dr. Doyle's eyes that made him step back.

"I'll clear it with the hospital administrator, Doctor," Calvin's mom said. "This is now officially a Dr. Catalyst task force case. The usual rules no longer apply. There will be two officers stationed outside Emmet's room at all times. No one is allowed inside without proper hospital identification. And Dr. Doyle will be staying here tonight with his son."

"But . . . that . . ." the doctor sputtered.

"That will be all, thank you," Dr. Geaux said.

The doctor tried to leave the room with a bit of dignity intact and failed. He scurried away and it was just the four of them.

"Well, he's back," Emmet said.

No one said anything. When the Muraecudas showed up, everyone gave him grief about how Dr. Catalyst had died in the swamp. And Emmet kept insisting he was alive. Eventually he was proven right. Dr. Catalyst had faked his death. Then he kept releasing more and more genetically altered species, and the only thing they all had in common was really big teeth. Huge teeth. Sharp. Quite pointy. Emmet had a suspicion that perhaps Dr. Catalyst secretly wanted to be some sort of evil dentist.

"There's no sign of the creature anywhere nearby," Dr. Geaux said. "Lieutenant Stukaczowski found some tracks near the canal behind your house. The photos we ran through the database don't match any animal we have on file. Which is pretty much any animal that leaves a track. The paw prints indicate it has retractable claws like a cat, but the rest of the footpads look canine. Canines don't catch food with claws. Cats do. This one looks like it can."

"Well, that's just great," Emmet said. "Teeth and claws."

"What's he trying to do this time?" Calvin piped up from the corner.

30

"What do you mean, son?" Dr. Geaux asked.

"I mean he made the Pterogators to eliminate the snakes. The Muraecudas were created to go after lionfish. Then he said the Blood Jackets were to show us what it was like when an invasive species was unleashed on humans. What is this creature after?" he asked.

"That's a good question. I wish I knew the answer," Dr. Doyle said.

"It's obvious," Emmet said. "Dr. Catalyst has one last invasive animal he wants to get rid of."

They all looked at him, waiting for clarification.

"Me."

5

DR. CATALYST DROVE HIS CAR SLOWLY THROUGH THE streets near the canal that ran behind the Doyle house. His tracking device showed his predator was slowly stalking along the waterway, stopping now and then and occasionally circling around to reverse course. Almost as if it wanted to return to finish the job.

But the Doyle home was undoubtedly a swarm of police and emergency vehicles. Now that Emmet was eliminated, Dr. Catalyst could retrieve the creature and return to his important work. He watched the monitor closely. It was vital to recapture his predator before the authorities discovered it.

Dr. Catalyst was overjoyed. Emmet Doyle was finished. Finally. Once Dr. Catalyst gathered up his new hybrid, there would be no one left to bother him. Hopefully the predator had finished Dr. Doyle as well. But even if not, he would be so distraught at the loss of his son, it was unlikely he would further interfere.

The red dot on the monitor moved south along the canal. Dr. Catalyst was on the other side. He needed to find a street with a bridge where he could cross over. Then he could activate the homing beacon and return the creature to his truck. After that, he would think on his next moves. Perhaps it could be retrained and used to curtail the spread of some other invasive species. He pondered that thought for a moment.

The night was quiet, and the streets deserted. Whatever else he might have done, Dr. Catalyst and his hybrid creatures had had a chilling effect on nighttime activity in Florida City. As he tracked the beast, he paused to tune the radio to an all-news station. The reporter was talking about an animal attack in the city. As he listened, Dr. Catalyst's smile turned to a frown.

"Here at WFCR we have learned that an unidentified animal has attacked a family in their home in Florida City. Details are incomplete, but we have confirmed that one person has been taken to a nearby hospital. The identity of the victim has not been revealed, but it is believed to be a young boy. Our sources indicate that he is in serious but stable condition. Authorities report that this as-yet-unidentified creature is extremely vicious and still at large. All Florida City residents are advised to remain indoors until further notice. We'll update our listeners as soon as we've learned more."

Dr. Catalyst pounded on the steering wheel in frustration, causing the van to swerve slightly in the road. He had to struggle to regain control of his emotions.

Unbelievable. How had this happened? In heaven's name, what did it take to rid the world of that little monster, Emmet Doyle? How did he manage, as slippery as an eel, to escape every single time?

It was nearly more than he could take. The time had come to rid himself of the Doyle brat once and for all. The sooner, the better.

Up ahead was a street leading to a bridge across the canal. Once across, the creature was only a few blocks away. It would follow the homing beacon to the van. When the beast was secured, he would return it to the training compound. He needed to think. There had to be a way.

Dr. Catalyst sped off into the night.

6

EMMET WAS RELEASED FROM THE HOSPITAL THE NEXT day and had to go immediately back to school. After the incident with the Blood Jackets, the State Health Department had gone through Tasker Middle School and cleaned out all of the Blood Jacket remains and . . . gunk . . . so classes could resume. "We have to recover and move on," the school official had said. Emmet said *pfft*. Let *them* recover and move on. The school officials hadn't been chased through the school by a screeching mass of biting, stinging horror-movie monsters.

When Emmet arrived at school that morning, it smelled clean. Like, über-clean. As if the entire building had been dipped in bleach. Calvin's mom dropped them off like usual. If she noticed that they were quiet and not talking, she didn't say anything. Emmet knew the way adults worked. If his dad had picked up on the fact that the two of them were squabbling, then Dr. Geaux, with her superior *momdar*, was perfectly aware of what was going on.

The antiseptic smell of the building was strangely reassuring. The day the Blood Jackets had attacked Emmet and his friends during the band concert, they'd had lunch like usual. Stuke noticed a bunch of Blood Jacket goop dripping out of one of the vents in the lunchroom. Remembering it made Emmet shudder. It was gray, gooey, and gross. Hopefully whoever cleaned up the school had been thorough. Emmet had half a mind to inspect the vents himself and make sure the Blood Jackets were really all gone.

"Emmet," Calvin said as they made their way through the crowded halls to their lockers.

"What?"

"We need to talk," he said.

"About what?"

"You know very well about what," Calvin said.

"Sorry, Calvin," Emmet said. "I'm not going to do this. When you came back from the swamp, you said you knew who Dr. Catalyst was. Since then you've been as silent as the Sphinx. I don't get it. But that guy is running around out there, doing real harm. Last night I thought I was going to die. But you haven't said anything." He walked faster, leaving Calvin behind. Emmet was working up a real head of steam, and he didn't want to blow up.

"I'm sorry about last night," Calvin said, hustling to keep up. "I'm really glad you're okay, Emmet. I don't . . . I haven't . . . I'm just not sure anymore. I thought I was, but I'm not. I have a reason, but I can't tell you."

"I'm sure you do," Emmet said. "You have a reason for everything you do."

By then Emmet had reached his locker and Calvin stopped, not saying anything. For a minute, Emmet thought Calvin would give up and head to his locker. It was about five minutes until the first bell. Calvin didn't like being late. But he stayed there while Emmet stowed his backpack and got his books organized for classes.

"Emmet. In the swamp . . . I thought I was sure . . . I mean . . . pretty sure. But the more I thought about it, I didn't have any real evidence. I still don't. And you can't go around accusing someone of something like this. . . ."

Emmet slammed his locker door shut.

"Spare me. If you know something about someone, all you need to do is tell your mom. They put the name and face out there. If the person is innocent, they come in and prove their innocence. The task force will just question them. If they're not the bad guy, they get to go home. I just don't see what the problem is. If they're guilty, then their name and face are all over the place, and maybe they get caught."

"I know . . . I . . . but . . ." Calvin stammered.

Emmet held up his hand, just like his dad had the night before.

"Save it," he said as the bell rang.

Emmet stormed off and went to class.

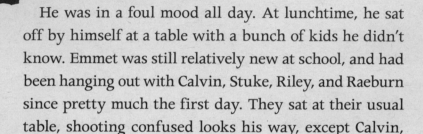

He was in a foul mood all day. At lunchtime, he sat off by himself at a table with a bunch of kids he didn't know. Emmet was still relatively new at school, and had been hanging out with Calvin, Stuke, Riley, and Raeburn since pretty much the first day. They sat at their usual table, shooting confused looks his way, except Calvin, who wore his usual stony face. Emmet knew they weren't getting anything out of him, either, but the others were content to give him some space.

The kids Emmet sat with were okay. They knew that his dad was working on the Dr. Catalyst case, and that was all they wanted to talk about. That, and whatever had happened to Dr. Newton. He still hadn't been found after allegedly being kidnapped, and everyone was assuming the worst. The school had extra counselors on hand to talk to kids who might be upset about it. A lot of students at Tasker liked Dr. Newton. He wasn't exactly Emmet's favorite teacher, but Emmet didn't want anything bad to happen to him. Unless he really was Dr. Catalyst. Then Emmet might be okay with a little maiming.

When all this mess had started, Emmet had been sure that Dr. Newton was really Dr. Catalyst. And if Dr. Catalyst could fake his own death, Dr. Newton could certainly have faked his own kidnapping and disappearance. But Calvin saw Dr. Catalyst up close at the aquarium, and his arm had been all mangled up from the not-so-unfortunate Pterogator accident that saved Emmet's life. Not long after, Dr. Newton had shown up at school with a cast conveniently covering the same arm. It was still suspicious to Emmet. The teacher had said it was because of a car accident.

Still, as the days went by, and the search for Dr. Newton become more and more hopeless, Emmet worried that maybe Dr. Newton hadn't been Dr. Catalyst after all. Maybe something bad had just happened to him.

These new kids were trying to be nice to Emmet, and he tried to be polite in return, but he wolfed down his lunch and excused himself way ahead of the bell.

His friends left him alone for the rest of the day. Emmet kind of sleepwalked through his classes. The afternoon seemed to drag, but the last bell finally rang. Calvin's mom always had a squad car from the Florida City PD drive them to Calvin's house after school, then the car would drive by every so often just to make sure they were okay. They also had to check in with Mrs. Clawson, Calvin's nearly blind and deaf next-door neighbor, and sometimes sitter. Their parents didn't want to keep them under lock and key, but Dr. Geaux was cautious.

"Emmet," Calvin said as they walked down the driveway toward his house.

"Don't even," Emmet said.

Calvin sighed. Mrs. Clawson was watering some flowers in her garden when they walked past. Usually she was in her living room watching game shows with the volume on the eardrum-busting setting.

"Hello, boys!" she said. Emmet and Calvin waved back and mumbled hello.

Calvin's mom allowed them to stay at the house by themselves until Emmet's dad picked him up after work. When Emmet wasn't busy not speaking to Calvin, they usually spent their time in Calvin's really cool tree house doing homework, or trying to come up with a way to catch Dr. Catalyst. Mostly Emmet tried to come up with the plans. Calvin didn't like falling behind on his homework.

But ever since the night Calvin had disappeared into the swamp, and Emmet had set out to find him and nearly gotten himself and his friends eaten alive in the process, they mostly passed the time ignoring each other. Not that Emmet wasn't grateful for Calvin showing up out of nowhere to rescue them. He just couldn't quite believe his once best friend would keep a secret as important as the identity of a deranged madman to himself.

These days Emmet usually stayed in the living room with Apollo, and avoided Calvin completely.

Except today.

Because today, when they walked in the front door, there was a man sitting on the couch in the living room. He was older, with shoulder-length black hair that was tinged with gray streaks. His kind face was lined and tan. When he spotted Calvin, he smiled. And Apollo was sitting calmly and comfortably in his lap. He looked a little bit like Calvin, and Emmet took a guess that they might be related. But he wasn't taking any chances.

"Who are —" Emmet shouted, dropping his backpack and digging into his pocket for his cell phone.

Calvin reached out and touched his arm. "It's okay, Emmet. It's okay."

"Hello, nephew," the old man said. His voice was deep. He sounded like someone who would narrate a nature documentary.

"Uncle Yaha?" Calvin asked. "What are you doing here?"

"You know what," the old man said. He looked down at Apollo and stroked his head. Apollo rolled over in the old man's lap, yawning and stretching out.

"Uncle?"

"It's time to put a stop to this, Calvin. Call your mother."

And Calvin did.

7

DR. CATALYST PULLED ALONG THE RUTTED LANE THAT LED to the gated compound where he kept this newest hybrid creature. It was only accessible by a long-abandoned park service road that led deep into the middle of the swamp. It was an ideal location. The expansive property was isolated, bordering a lake along its northern edge. There he had a dock with an airboat at the ready; the lake fed a river leading directly to the Taylor Slough and gave him quick access to many of his other hideouts.

An automatic gate opened. Dr. Catalyst pulled through, making sure it closed behind him. Once inside the barn he backed the van up to the containment pen where the hybrid was usually caged. The barred steel enclosure had an opening for a door cut into the barn wall. It allowed the creature to roam the acreage as it pleased. A twelve-foot-high fence enclosed the property. The fence also extended six feet into the ground, and the top of it was covered in razor wire. Dr. Catalyst did not worry about his predator escaping.

The hybrid bounded out of the van, through the pen, and out into the open fields beyond the barn. Dr. Catalyst watched it prowl along the land from the barn window, growling and barking as it went. It was a magnificent beast. Some trick or other unforeseen circumstance must have kept it from completing its mission. Dr. Catalyst knew from experience how slippery Emmet Doyle could be.

Now that his first effort was foiled, Dr. Catalyst needed to come up with some other way of loosing the creature on Emmet. As he thought, he realized his mistake. All of his former creatures had been designed for particular purposes. To restore balance to the Everglades and the environment. Except for the Blood Jackets, which had been unleashed to teach his enemies a lesson.

Once he mastered the complexities of recombining the DNA and splicing genes for each species, creating clones had been fairly simple. It just took time and resources. And the creatures he created did work as he intended, until the little horror that was Emmet Doyle had shown up.

Now that he had created a creature for the sole purpose of stopping Emmet, he recognized the flaw in his plan. His other creatures had been bred in large numbers. It required the resources of the entire task force to maintain order, contain the animals, and manage the crisis. With just one creature, the authorities would focus on keeping Emmet safe. Dr. Catalyst paused to consider this for a moment.

He'd already kidnapped Dr. Doyle. He had even snatched Emmet's monstrous dog. Once they figured out this hybrid was a solitary creation with a single target, security around Emmet would be tightened. The task force would expect Dr. Catalyst to follow his pattern and snatch Emmet, using him as leverage to meet some demand or another. Ha! If they only knew. All he wanted was to get rid of the annoying little twerp.

Therefore, he needed to break the pattern.

If he wanted his creature to succeed, he would need to do more extensive planning. No protection or surveillance detail was perfect. Despite their best efforts, unless he was put in lockdown or held in a castle somewhere, Emmet would at some point be alone and exposed. He could be separated from his protectors.

Dr. Catalyst studied the creature as it stalked through the trees and grass of his property. It dawned on him that, like they had been from the very beginning, the hybrids he'd created were his greatest resources. If he could use the creature to instill fear in the population of Florida City, then the task force would be compelled to withdraw their protection of Emmet and focus on stopping the threat.

With the authorities occupied elsewhere, he would strike. He would find a way to separate Emmet from his safety net. Then he would arrange a meeting between the troublesome child and his newest pet.

That was the best way. The smart way. Dr. Catalyst smiled.

The barn was where he now slept and worked. All of his equipment had been moved inside. The interior no longer looked or functioned like a barn, except for the one pen for his creature. One of the rooms was set up with his computers, lab equipment, and a workstation. The wall was completely covered by a large flat-screen, high-definition computer monitor.

Sitting down at the desk, he ran his fingers over the keyboard, pulling a map of Florida City up on the screen. It was time to get to work.

It was time for vengeance.

8

THINGS HAPPENED FAST. CALVIN CALLED HIS MOM, AND she and Emmet's dad arrived about thirty minutes later, both trying to look like they were calm. Like they hadn't just rushed to the house as fast as they could. As soon as she walked in the door, Emmet sensed that Dr. Geaux and Calvin's great-uncle were . . . not exactly unfriendly, but maybe they didn't send each other birthday cards, either.

He remembered her telling him that it had been difficult for her and Calvin's dad when they were first married. Dr. Geaux was not a Seminole, and Lucas Geaux's family had difficulty with that fact. Emmet found it hard to think that anyone wouldn't welcome

Dr. Geaux into their family, but he also knew families were complicated sometimes.

"Hello, Yaha," she said. Her voice was wary.

"Hello, Rosalita," the old man said. "You look well." Apollo jumped off his lap, and Yaha stood.

"It's been a long time," she said. "This is Dr. Benton Doyle, and this is his son, Emmet."

"I have had the pleasure of speaking to Emmet while we waited for you," Yaha said. "Dr. Doyle, it's nice to meet you." He nodded at Dr. Doyle but stood there with his hands behind his back, kind of stiff and unmoving. It was all very odd.

Dr. Geaux waited for a few moments, as if she was waiting for Yaha to speak, but he seemed content to stand in the middle of the living room and stare at everyone. Nobody said anything, until Apollo suddenly seemed to realize that Emmet's dad was there and went over and yipped in greeting. Dr. Doyle knelt and scratched him behind the ears. Somehow it broke the ice.

"Why are you here, Yaha?" Dr. Geaux asked.

"I am here to help," he said.

"Help? Help who? With what?" Emmet and his dad were watching them talk, their heads going back and forth like they were observing a tennis match. Calvin was standing by the far end of the couch, squirming. Emmet had never seen him squirm before. It was like

Calvin couldn't find something to comfortably stare at. His eyes traveled all over the room, but he wasn't looking at anyone.

"With the one who calls himself Dr. Catalyst," he said.

Dr. Geaux and Dr. Doyle were taken aback.

"You have information about Dr. Catalyst?" she asked.

"Yes," he said. "I do. In fact, I know who he is."

Dr. Geaux didn't react like Emmet expected. He thought she might take Calvin's uncle somewhere to have him interrogated. But she just crossed her arms, and her face took on an expression that was hard to describe. Like she didn't trust him. Or like she resented him for standing in her house right now. Emmet couldn't be sure.

"So tell me, Yaha. Who is Dr. Catalyst?"

"You might want to sit down," he said.

"I'll stand, thank you," she said.

"Very well. This will be hard for you to understand," he said.

"Try me," she said.

"What I am about to tell you, I have told no one except Calvin, when he came to visit me on the reservation," he said.

Dr. Geaux tried not to show anything, but the disappointment on her face could not be hidden. Emmet saw

Calvin sag from the corner of his eye. Dr. Geaux stood up straighter, putting her hands on her hips. Her eyes bored into Calvin, but he looked down at the floor.

"Look at me," she said.

He did.

"You did this? You went to the rez to see Yaha?"

"Yes, ma'am," Calvin mumbled.

"Why?"

"Because I had to know," he said.

"Know what?" Dr. Geaux was almost trembling. Emmet couldn't tell if she was mad or nervous or what. His dad reached out and put his hand on her shoulder.

"I had to find out if Dr. Catalyst was . . . is . . . my grandfather," Calvin said.

Dr. Geaux sat down.

9

IT WAS DARK NOW.

The Geaux house was on a small cul-de-sac. The backyard was fenced in, but a few yards beyond the fence ran a small creek. Usually at this time of the evening, the sounds of night creatures filled the air. Tree frogs peeped, alligators bellowed, and birds called to each other as they settled in their nests.

But tonight it was silent.

Tonight there was a new, strange predator in their midst.

The beast stalked slowly along the bank of the creek. It worked its nose over the wet, muddy ground. Somewhere nearby was the scent. It was very faint, but it was there. The prey was nearby. Or had been recently.

It paused a moment to drink from the creek. A small log lay just above the surface and a turtle, spying the predator, dived into the water. It growled then, and other animals could be heard splashing into the creek and scurrying away into the underbrush.

Nose to the ground, it moved farther along the creek. It saw lights in the houses beyond the fenced-in back-yards. The fences were placed there to keep the alligators out, but presented no obstacle for an animal with its climbing and leaping ability.

The hair on the back of its neck stood on end. Its head snapped up. It smelled the prey's scent. Close by and strong. It followed the smell to the base of the fence. The fence was made of cypress planks, but it was not nearly tall enough to prevent the predator from leaping to the top of it. Clambering down the other side, it found itself in an empty backyard, except for the trees.

One of the trees was covered in the scent. The beast sniffed at the base. There was dog smell here, but the scent of the prey rose upward, which was confusing. The creature stood on its hind legs, inhaling repeatedly. With a powerful leap, it climbed up the trunk, and the smell grew stronger. The prey was not here now, but this must be his lair, for his odor was very prevalent here.

The creature's claws dug into the trunk. Above it, in the branches, was a small wooden structure with a hole cut into the floor. It climbed inside, and was overwhelmed by the scent. It was everywhere — along the floorboards and in the corners. But the prey himself was not here. The predator smelled the air and caught the scent again. The wooden tree box had screens, and through one of them the creature saw a house. Lights were on, and there were humans inside. From here, their odors combined, but the creature inhaled deeply and . . . there it was. The smell it sought.

The prey was inside the house.

Quickly it exited the wooden box and descended the tree. It let out a low growl as it stalked across the lawn toward the house. Carefully and cautiously it crept toward the rear door. The smell was much stronger now. It triggered a release of saliva in its mouth, as it thought of the delicious food it received from the man whenever it found the source of the smell.

There was a stone floor in the grass that led to the door of the house. The hybrid silently crossed it, until it could peer in through the glass. There were several humans inside. Now the predator began to plan. The smell was inside. The smell meant food.

The creature backed up, studying the outlines of the humans inside the house. With a mighty roar, it reared back and charged forward, leaping toward the glass.

It was time to attack.

10

EMMET STARED AT CALVIN. HE COULDN'T HELP IT. HIS jaw was almost on his chest.

"Did you just say your grandfather? Dr. Catalyst is your grandfather?" Something wasn't right here. "I thought he was dead."

"So did I," Calvin mumbled, his head down.

"Wait. Wait a minute," Dr. Geaux was saying. "You can't possibly mean this. Lucas's father died in the swamp. Years ago."

"I am afraid that is not true, Rosalita," Yaha said. "He is very much alive."

"You're lying!" Dr. Geaux said. She walked over to Calvin and stood behind him, with her arms around him. Like she wanted to protect him from some awful truth.

"Would that it were so, but I'm not."

"How do you know this?" Dr. Doyle asked. "And if you know it, why didn't you say anything until now? Do you know what this man has done? The damage he's caused? The people he's hurt? If you knew —"

Yaha held up his hand, cutting him off.

"I know it's true because he came to me some months ago, after he was injured in a confrontation with one of his . . . Pterogators, I believe he called them? I provided him with treatment." There was something about Yaha — something Emmet couldn't quite put his finger on — that made him think the old man was telling the truth. Yaha stood there in the living room, ramrod straight, and acted almost irritated that anyone would question him.

He was also starting to make Emmet a little angry.

"What do you mean, 'treatment'?" Dr. Doyle asked.

"Yaha is, or rather was, a medical doctor," Dr. Geaux said.

"Yes. I am a doctor. Retired. I served in the army in Vietnam as a battalion aid surgeon. I returned home to run the central clinic on the reservation for many years. Now I am retired and live at my camp in the Everglades. The man you call Dr. Catalyst came to me injured, bleeding, almost dead. I treated his wounds and nursed him back to health."

Now Dr. Geaux was furious. She had an olive complexion to begin with, and was always tanned from being out in the sun a lot. Now you could see the red showing through on her cheeks, a bright red that was growing brighter by the minute.

"Did you know what he was doing? What he'd done? Kidnapping? Releasing these creatures? Why didn't you stop him? Turn him in? People have been hurt, Yaha!" She had moved past furious, straight to seething.

"Yes. And it is regrettable. At first, I didn't turn him in because I agreed with him," he said quietly.

"You . . . what?" Dr. Geaux was flabbergasted.

"No one can argue that the Everglades aren't being destroyed by man," he said. "The current problems with pythons and boa constrictors are just the latest. The River of Grass has suffered mismanagement and outright destruction for many years. Dr. Catalyst — the man you would call my brother-in-law — has been seeking to restore nature's balance in his own way. But as I considered it, I grew to think that while he may have his heart in the right place, his methods are not sustainable. They will only cause further damage. He has lost his way. When Calvin came to me with the photo and his questions, I answered them as best I could. But the more I thought of it — about Calvin, about Philip — I realized I could not allow him to continue as Dr. Catalyst."

"Well, thank you so much," Emmet said. He couldn't help it. Now he was furious, boiling-mad, someone-better-stop-him-before-he-does-something-he'll-regret angry. This Yaha person just sat out there, knowing all along who Dr. Catalyst was, and probably how to find him, and kept it a secret? Oh. No. Way.

Yaha looked at Emmet, and for a moment Emmet saw something flash across his eyes. It wasn't anger or regret. It was shame. But it was only there for a brief instant, and then it was gone.

Emmet's hands were balled into fists. He stalked across the carpet until he was right in the old man's face. "He kidnapped my father! He stole my dog! I got disgusting Blood Jacket goop all over me! And you knew! I don't care what you thought about balance. My dad and Dr. Geaux and a bunch of other people have been working around the clock to fix this mess. People's lives have been put in danger. And you knew? You should be arrested! In fact, Dr. Geaux, arrest him! Take him downtown and beat him with a nightstick until he tells us everything! And —" Emmet felt arms on his shoulders pulling him back.

"Whoa, son," his dad said, trying to gently lead him away. "Cool off. This isn't getting us anywhere."

"I don't blame you for being angry," Yaha said.

"Oh, I'm not angry. I'm incensed." Then Emmet remembered Calvin. He had a role here, too. He spun on his friend.

"And you knew? All this time?" Emmet couldn't see himself, but he was sure he was turning purple by now.

"I thought I did. But with all respect to my elder, these are not the things he told me," Calvin said.

"What? You're not making sense at all. Why is no one making any sense here?" Emmet was trying to get free of his dad's grip, but Dr. Doyle just held him a little tighter.

Calvin sighed and tried to explain. "I had a photo of some men. It was in a journal that belonged to my father. I found it after he died. They were out in a camp in the Everglades. One of them sort of looked like the man we saw at the school when the Blood Jackets attacked. Uncle Yaha was in the photo, too. I went to the reservation to find out the identity of the man in the photo. He told me it was my grandfather. Not that it was Dr. Catalyst. He told me none of what he's said here tonight. I thought and thought about it. And I began to think maybe my grandfather was alive. My dad told me Grandfather was very smart. He went to college and had a PhD in microbiology. When he lived on the reservation, he fought long and hard with the state and federal government over saving the Everglades. But I couldn't get around the fact that my dad was convinced he'd died in the swamp. No one knew the Everglades better than Dad. He wouldn't make a mistake like that. So the more I thought about it, I couldn't just come out and accuse someone of being Dr. Catalyst — someone who was supposed to be long dead — because we caught a fleeting glimpse of a guy in a hallway."

"Calvin is telling the truth," Yaha said. "I told him nothing about his grandfather being alive. And he is correct in that no one knew the swamp better than his father, Lucas Geaux. Except one person — his *grand*-father, Philip Geaux. I have come here now to tell you the rest of the story."

Emmet wanted to punch something, but he never got the opportunity. Apollo started barking and running around in circles, back and forth between the patio doors and the living room. Crazy barking. Like he had a couple of nights ago.

"Apollo . . ." Dr. Doyle said.

Then the patio door exploded in a cascade of broken glass.

11

SOMETHING BIG, FURRY, AND ANGRY CAME TUMBLING through the shattered doorway. It was like a monster from a horror movie had jumped off the screen and landed in the dining room.

It growled and tensed its body, ready to spring.

Emmet was frozen in place. All he could see was a giant set of jaws headed for him. And for a brief second, he wondered, *Why me?* But somewhere deep in his gut, Emmet knew that Dr. Catalyst had sent this creature after him alone. Unless it was captured or killed, there would be no stopping it.

There was shouting and barking in the background, but it seemed far away. The world around Emmet appeared to move in slow motion. Voices and sounds took forever to reach his thoughts.

The animal was big. At least two hundred pounds, if Emmet had to guess. It stood there growling, its mouth open and full of giant teeth. It crouched low to the ground, hate-filled eyes pointed straight at Emmet, ready to spring. It probably would have killed him right then, if not for Apollo.

Apollo weighed maybe twenty-five pounds, if he hadn't had a haircut. He was half poodle, a breed known for its intelligence, speed, and agility, and half schnauzer, a breed known for being ferocious and territorial. The beast that shattered the dining room door outweighed Apollo by at least 175 pounds. When they'd lived in Montana, Emmet's dad used to chuckle whenever Apollo would want to take on a critter bigger and probably more ferocious than he was. He would say, "It's not the size of the dog in the fight. It's the size of the fight in the dog."

Apollo had defended Emmet the other night, when this thing almost got into their house. Only Emmet's lucky grab had kept the dog from getting hurt. But Apollo was out of reach this time, and now he set himself between Emmet and the creature. The schnoodle crouched low to the ground. His muscles tensed and he puffed himself up, growling and barking like Emmet had never heard him. He was also getting ready to attack. It was like he was telling the giant intruder to bring it on.

His presence seemed to confuse the beast momentarily. It stared at him for a second, growling a full-throated growl. Its fur was all brown but spotted in places, and its head was shaped funny, like a dog and cat mixed together. Whatever it was, it was terrifying. And Emmet still couldn't move. His fight-or-flight reflex had discovered a third option. Fright.

All of this felt like it took hours to happen, but in reality it was merely seconds. Then the beast, deciding Apollo was no threat, turned its eyes back toward Emmet. Emmet heard Dr. Geaux calling his name.

"Emmet! Move! Move!" she shouted. He didn't know why she wanted him to move, and besides, he couldn't. Because of the being-petrified thing. It felt like the creature would devour him in an instant if he moved.

But all that didn't matter, because in the next moment the beast launched itself over Apollo, straight toward him. This was it. All he could do was close his eyes and wait for death.

But it never came.

Emmet felt something brush past him and heard the creature howl in confusion and rage. He opened his eyes to find Yaha and the beast grappling with each other a few feet away from him.

Yaha wrapped his arms around the creature's body, and they tumbled to the floor. The old man cried out in agony when the creature sank its fangs into his shoulder, but he didn't let go.

Apollo charged into the fray. He sank his own teeth into the cat's hind leg and bit down hard. The creature yelped in pain, and Yaha yanked his shoulder free when it opened its mouth. It flicked its leg and tried to shake Apollo free, but the little mutt would not give in. If anything, Apollo seemed to bite down harder. Yaha leapt in, trying to pin its jaws shut with his bare hands. Emmet may have been ticked off at him a few minutes ago, but he had to admit Calvin's uncle had courage.

Dr. Geaux yelled at Emmet to move. Now he did, rushing forward to grab Apollo. He grasped the dog around his body and pulled, but he still would not let go.

"No, Emmet! Back up!" he heard her shout.

"Emmet, no! Run!" someone else yelled. Possibly his dad. But he couldn't leave his dog. It was all he could think of. The thought of saving Apollo had broken Emmet's paralysis.

"Apollo! OFF!" Emmet shouted. But the schnoodle was nearly mad with rage. Yaha was taking a beating. The creature was clawing and biting him as he tried to stay on top of it, pinning it to the ground. Dr. Geaux appeared in Emmet's line of vision. She had her sidearm out and pointed it at the beast, but couldn't shoot because she might hit Yaha.

Emmet's dad was suddenly next to him, trying to help pry Apollo loose. The beast itself was in a fury, and it kicked out with one leg. Its claws raked across Dr. Doyle's chest. Emmet's dad screamed in pain.

"Dad!" Emmet hollered as his dad slumped to the ground, blood seeping from his chest.

In the interim, the creature managed to flip Yaha off him. The old man flew into the dining room, sending the table and chairs crashing in all directions. Emmet was pretty sure he was unconscious. The rug around him was covered in blood. Apollo let go, and Emmet fell backward onto his rear end, with Apollo clutched in his arms. He was still wiggling, snarling, and barking, trying desperately to get back into the battle.

With Yaha thrown off, the creature leapt at Dr. Geaux before she could react and bit down hard on her arm. She yelled in agony, and the gun fell free, spinning away from her. Emmet tried to scramble to his feet. Everyone needed his help. But the creature's head snapped around when he moved. It started toward him, and he squeezed Apollo tighter.

Emmet couldn't stand. He tried to scrabble backward. The strange beast took its time now. It stared at him and sniffed the air, growling. There was nothing but empty space between them. Nothing Emmet could use as a weapon, or anything to hide behind. It slowly stalked toward him. Apollo was still barking, and all Emmet could think to do was shout and holler, trying to keep it away. Closer and closer it came, until its mouth and jaw were just a few feet away. One jump, and it would be upon him. Emmet glanced frantically around for any escape. There was no way out.

In all the chaos, and his extreme desire to not get eaten, Emmet had forgotten all about Calvin. He shouldn't have. He heard a weird whooshing sound and the creature's face instantly turned snow-white.

Emmet's mind couldn't process what was happening, but the genetic freak growled and shook its head, trying to clear its eyes. But more white stuff came flying from behind him. The beast stood frozen in place, unsure of what had happened to it.

A gunshot sounded, startling the creature and causing Emmet to scream loudly. Emmet glanced over to find that Dr. Geaux had pulled herself across the floor to her weapon and was now sitting up with one arm hanging limply at her side. There was an ugly trail of blood behind her. She fired into the air again, and Calvin gave the beast another blast of whatever he was using. Some kind of magic monster repellent. Whatever it was caused the creature to turn and sprint out the door. Dr. Geaux fired one more shot at it, but she must've missed. Calvin flew past Emmet, holding a can of wasp-and-hornet spray. He kept pulling the trigger as he ran through the door.

"Calvin! No!" Emmet heard Dr. Geaux shout. But she had nothing left and slumped backward to the floor. Emmet was certain she was unconscious. He struggled to his knees, still holding the squirming Apollo. Calvin reappeared in the doorway.

"It's gone," he said. Emmet released Apollo, who charged to his dad, lying still and motionless on the ground. He licked at his face, whining, as if begging him to wake up.

Calvin was calling 9-1-1 on the house phone. Emmet heard him ask for police and an ambulance. There were three badly injured people in the room, and Emmet didn't know which one to help first.

Dr. Geaux looked like she was in worse shape than his dad, and Calvin was already headed to his uncle's side. Emmet crawled across the floor to Dr. Geaux. Her arm was bleeding badly and her eyes were closed. He peeled off the polo shirt he was wearing and pressed it against her wounded arm.

His dad groaned and tried to sit up.

"Dad, be still," Emmet said. "You're injured."

Calvin knelt beside his uncle Yaha. From the look of things, he was in the worst shape of all three. His blood was everywhere. Calvin glanced up at Emmet.

"Wasp spray?" Emmet asked.

"We always keep a can in the kitchen closet," he said.

"Of course you do," Emmet said.

The sirens grew louder as they drew nearer. The boys got busy trying to keep everyone alive.

12

ONCE AGAIN, DR. CATALYST POUNDED ON THE STEERING wheel in frustration. Finding it to be an unsatisfactory release of his anger and rage, he grabbed the Maglite flashlight on the seat and slammed it into the dashboard over and over. Finally, he tossed it onto the floorboards and slumped back into the driver's seat.

The plan had been set up perfectly. During his reconnaissance, he had studied and followed Calvin and Emmet as they left school and returned home. He watched the police patrols who protected them and looked for patterns. The two boys very rarely left the house once home, and the so-called babysitter next door was no threat.

It grew dark early this time of year, which gave Dr. Catalyst time to release the creature before Dr. Geaux and Dr. Doyle arrived home for the evening. At first he'd wrestled with indecision over including young Calvin in his vendetta. It was Emmet Doyle he was after. It was Emmet who'd ruined everything. Perhaps Calvin would survive. If not, then he would be collateral damage in his crusade to save the Everglades.

It was dark when Dr. Catalyst released the Swamp Cat — as he'd started calling it — at the creek. The location was isolated, yet close enough to the Geaux house for it to pick up Emmet's scent. The creature was now familiar with its mission and comfortable tracking the boy. When the vehicle's rear door was opened and it was freed from the cage, it leapt to the ground and immediately began hunting.

He'd watched as it traveled along the creek, until it disappeared into the darkness. Dr. Catalyst could still hear it stalking through the undergrowth near the bank and every so often its growl carried through the night air. When there was no longer any sight or sound of the Swamp Cat, he hopped in the delivery van and drove to a spot on the street near the house, where he would have a view of the events. As he watched, he was nearly giddy with anticipation. But then the minutes ticked by, and he grew nervous waiting. In his rearview mirror, he saw a police car turning onto the street. He ducked down until it passed by.

Dr. Catalyst monitored the Swamp Cat's progress on his tablet. According to the tracker, it was now along the bank, nearing the Geaux house. Silently he willed the beast to move faster.

Headlights flashed in his mirror. He slumped in the seat again but sat up in alarm when a silver Buick pulled into the Geaux driveway. Dr. Geaux and Dr. Doyle hurried out of the car and rushed inside. Glancing at the tablet, the red dot indicated the creature was now in the backyard. Had the boys spotted it and called to alert their parents? Should he activate the homing beacon and recapture it?

No. Unlikely. Emmet Doyle and Calvin Geaux were smart and resourceful. If they had seen the Swamp Cat, they would have called 9-1-1 immediately. Something else was happening here. The tracker still showed the cat in the backyard. What was going on? Was there some alarm, or motion sensor that might have confused or delayed the beast? Rolling the window down, he strained to listen, but could hear nothing.

He waited, sweat forming on his brow and running down into his eyes. Then the red dot on the tablet rapidly moved forward. By the map on the screen, the Swamp Cat was inside the house!

"Yes!" he shouted. "Yes!"

His joy turned to immediate concern a few seconds later when he heard a gunshot, followed quickly by another. Had Dr. Geaux shot the Swamp Cat? No. How could this be? The animal was too fast and ferocious for normal human reflexes. Remembering to look at the monitor, he was relieved to find the red dot moving away from the house. It crossed the backyard, probably jumping the fence, and was now progressing steadily along the creek.

Dr. Catalyst started the truck and sped to the spot where he had released the Swamp Cat. He activated the homing beacon, knowing the animal would return to the van. The beacon emitted the scent it had been trained on, and the van was filled with food.

He waited.

The tracker showed the red dot moving in his direction. Taking his position behind the open rear door, he kept one eye on the tablet and one on the darkness, but it was still shocking when the powerful animal burst out of the underbrush. It vaulted into the pen and Dr. Catalyst quickly lowered the cage door. He jumped up into the cargo bay and turned on his flashlight. The creature snarled at the light, stalking back and forth in the cage, but there were no signs of blood. It did not appear wounded, although its face and the fur around its shoulders were covered with some strange white substance.

Dr. Catalyst was relieved the Swamp Cat had not been seriously injured. In the distance he heard sirens. Lots of sirens. It was time to find out what had happened. He drove back to his spot on the street just in time to see several police cars and ambulances arrive.

As he watched, he put on a hat and turned up the collar on his jacket. Neighbors were exiting their houses into the street to investigate the commotion. It would not do to be recognized.

A few minutes later, paramedics emerged from the house, with someone on a gurney. Moments later came another one. Calvin Geaux stood next to it. Part of Dr. Catalyst was glad his creature had spared the kid. It was not entirely his fault the Doyle brat had corrupted him.

Dr. Catalyst held his breath, waiting for his moment. There would be a smaller body on a gurney, covered in a sheet, and the weeping, hysterical Dr. Doyle walking next to it. Finally he would have his victory.

When the next set of paramedics emerged, he sat stunned at the wheel of the van. Emmet Doyle, illuminated by the flashing emergency lights, was walking next to it. It appeared he didn't have a scratch on him. It must have been his father who was injured. Emmet stepped into the ambulance and it pulled away.

"No!" he shouted, pounding his fist on the steering wheel again. "No! What does it take to kill this kid!?" Nothing he tried worked. Emmet Doyle was a magician!

And that was how he found himself, a few hours later, driving toward Miami. Looking in the mirror, he checked his disguise. He had dyed his hair blond with an over-the-counter coloring kit and wore a fake mustache. Now dressed in a police uniform, he was driving a Florida City police cruiser.

One way or another, it was time to end this.

13

EMMET'S DAD, DR. GEAUX, AND CALVIN'S UNCLE YAHA all had to be airlifted to South Miami Hospital. It was the same hospital Stuke had been taken to after the Muraecuda bit him. Emmet and Calvin sat together in the OR waiting room. He thought it was the most appropriately named room ever. Waiting. Room. The minutes dragged. There was an old-fashioned clock hanging on the wall, right above a row of extremely uncomfortable chairs. He swore he could hear the seconds ticking, but the minute hand moved like a glacier.

When they'd first arrived, he and Calvin both paced back and forth. But they eventually paced themselves out, and now sat across from each other. The seats had stiff backs and thin cushions. They couldn't be less inviting, but it didn't really matter. There was no way Emmet could feel comfortable under the circumstances, anyway.

Stuke's dad, a Florida City police lieutenant, was on the Dr. Catalyst task force. He and his wife notified the paramedics that they were bringing Stuke, Riley, and Raeburn to the hospital for moral support. Mrs. Clawson was watching Apollo. For now it was just the two of them. Waiting. In the waiting room. After he stopped pacing, Calvin sat in a chair, all stiff and rigid. Emmet knew he was worried about his mom. And while he never got a chance to hear the complete story about Dr. Catalyst being his grandfather, now was probably not the time to have it out with him. Now was the time to be a friend. Even if he was still a little ticked off.

"All right, I get it," Emmet said. "I don't agree with what you did. Holding back information like that. It could have saved us from almost getting eaten by that giant cat-dog creature. But now I understand why you had questions. I mean, how old were you the last time you saw your grandfather alive?"

"I never saw him," Calvin said. His voice was tinged with sadness.

"So if you haven't seen him in that long, then you . . . Wait, never?" Emmet suddenly processed what he'd heard. Calvin had never met his own grandfather. "I'm sorry, Calvin. I didn't know that." Now he felt even worse. Calvin was a smart, brave, honest kid. Emmet was starting to understand why he was reluctant to speak up. At least a part of him was.

Calvin shrugged. "My dad told me he died before I was born."

"What made you recognize him in the hallway at school?" Emmet asked.

"I don't know. That picture . . . the one from my dad's journal . . . I've probably studied it a thousand times. I've always wanted to be like my dad, living in a camp in the swamp, catching fish and gators and stuff. And all the time we spent out there — flying around on his boat — he would tell me about how his dad taught him everything about the Everglades. Like he was going to teach me. Only my dad died before he could teach me everything he knew.

"Then I saw this guy for a brief second in the hallway, and it kind of jolted me. He looked just like the man in the photo."

Calvin sighed and leaned back in the chair. "My dad showed me the picture a few times. It was the only one he had of his father. But I never knew where he kept it. After I found it in his journal I'd just look at it sometimes, you know? And wonder. I memorized the face. Wondered what he would be like if he were still alive. Then I saw him in the hallway. . . . Anyway, I had to be sure. Was I remembering the right person? Maybe I'd forgotten. I knew Mom would be hard to convince. So I took *Dragonfly One* and went to visit Uncle Yaha. I just asked if one of the men in the photo was my grandfather. He asked me why I wanted to know, but I wouldn't tell him. Finally he told me yes, it was. I swear he never told me anything about Grand . . . about Dr. Catalyst coming to him. Honest, Emmet. He never did."

"I believe you, Calvin," Emmet said. And he did.

"I was on my way back home when I found you and Rilcy and Raeburn stranded in the swamp. I was going to tell my mom. But I thought about it. My grandfather was dead. How could he be Dr. Catalyst? With no proof of anything except my quick glance down a hallway? What if I was wrong? My mom . . . she tries so hard to get Yaha and the rest of my father's family to accept her. She does it for my sake. What if I was wrong? They would never forgive her for dishonoring the family name. She'd already lost my dad. I couldn't . . . After a while, I just stopped thinking I saw what I thought I saw," he said.

"So how did your grandfather become Dr. Catalyst?" Emmet asked him.

Calvin shook his head. "I don't know. I was counting on Uncle Yaha to fill in some of the details. My dad very rarely spoke about his father, except when we were on the River of Grass, when he would say his dad taught him this or that. I guess they had some kind of a falling-out. All I know is he was really smart. He studied microbiology somewhere and was a top student. I went to the library and looked up newspaper articles about him. He once tried to run for a seat on the tribal council but didn't get elected. Before he died, he was always working with some group or another to save the Everglades. In all the articles about him he would rave on and on about the environment being destroyed. He hated the government, developers, even the tribe, for destroying the Everglades."

"Sounds like our man," Emmet said.

"But then he died."

"Or not," Emmet said.

"Or not," Calvin echoed resignedly.

A woman in a white coat bustled into the waiting room. Nurse Hernandez had helped them when they arrived at the hospital.

"What's happening? What's going on?" Emmet asked, as both he and Calvin scrambled to their feet.

"Emmet, your dad is going to be okay. He has some deep lacerations on his chest, and one of the creature's claws punctured a lung. That's a pretty serious injury. He lost some blood, but he'll recover. It'll be a few days in the hospital. He's on a heavy dose of antibiotics, as we need to guard against infection." She turned to Calvin.

"Calvin, your mom is okay," she said. "The bite broke her arm and cut some ligaments and tendons. She's still in surgery, but we've got two great surgeons working on her right now. Dr. Geaux will probably need a lot of physical therapy, but the important thing is she's going to be all right."

"What about my uncle Yaha?" Calvin asked, a wave of relief washing over him that his mother was going to be okay.

Her faced changed. She got a lot more serious.

"I don't know yet," she said. "Your uncle took the worst of the attack. He lost a lot of blood, and he has bites and puncture wounds everywhere. He has an entire team of surgeons working on him right now, and his condition is still critical. He's going to be in the OR for quite a while. I'm sorry to give you boys this news when you're here all alone. Do you have anyone coming to stay with you? Any family? It will be some time before you can see your parents, I'm afraid."

"We have friends coming," Emmet said. "Including Lieutenant Stukaczowski from the Dr. Catalyst task force. They're on the way from Florida City. They should be here anytime now. Will we be able to see our parents as soon as —"

He never got to finish. The earsplitting Klaxon sound of the hospital fire alarm interrupted him. Strobe lights flashed and the noise pounded the air like a hammer.

"What the . . ." Emmet said.

"I don't know. But we're going to have to evacuate," Nurse Hernandez said.

"What!? But what about our parents? What about the operating rooms?" He was scared now.

"Don't worry. It's probably a false alarm. It happens all the time. But even if it isn't, your parents and uncle will be okay. The operating rooms are sealed and heavily protected by fire-suppression systems. We'll be able to stabilize them and evacuate them to a nearby OR in an adjacent building," she said.

A voice came over the speaker system. "Attention. Attention. We have a fire emergency. This is not a drill. All personnel please execute patient-evacuation-plan Alpha. This is not a drill. Repeat. This is a fire emergency. Execute evacuation-plan Alpha."

"Okay, boys, I need to start moving patients, and you need to leave the building. Use the stairs and go out the exit right away." Nurse Hernandez sped away, her lab coat flapping behind her.

Calvin had a worried look on his face, but Emmet knew there was no way he would ignore a fire alarm. They hurried to the stairway door, pushed it open, and started their descent.

The farther down they went, the more something started tugging at a corner of Emmet's brain. A crazy genetic freak attacks them and a few hours later, while they're in the hospital waiting for their parents to get out of surgery, a fire alarm goes off?

What were the odds?

Something didn't feel right.

14

DR. CATALYST STRODE THROUGH THE LOBBY OF THE hospital. It was always amazing to him how easy it was to get into and out of places if you assumed the identity of someone in authority. His Florida City police uniform gave him entry to the entire hospital. No one stopped or questioned him.

On the drive to Miami, he had contemplated how he could get his hands on Emmet. Going straight into the hospital and asking for him would arouse suspicion. Worse, there would be security cameras, and a record of him asking. The boy might also be under watch by security or other police officials, and they would not be so easily fooled by his disguise. He didn't want to charge into a gaggle of police officers. The best option would be to get the hospital empty and have Emmet outside, where he might have a chance to separate him from those watching him.

The ideal way to do that would be to create some kind of emergency. The easiest emergency would be a fire alarm. But he couldn't just pull the fire alarm. Hospitals had sophisticated fire-detection-and-suppression systems. Once they determined it was a false alarm, they would simply shut it off. Which meant he would need to start an actual fire. But he had to choose a spot carefully. He did not want to unnecessarily hurt anyone. Once word got out that Emmet was missing, he would receive enough bad publicity. Setting fire to a hospital would not win any followers to his cause. But the Doyle brat's interference had gone on long enough.

Dr. Catalyst parked the cruiser in a parking garage adjacent to the hospital. He studied a map of the interior of the building on his tablet. Looking closely at the layout of the place, he immediately found the ideal location for his decoy fire. He entered the building through a side entrance, carrying a small duffel bag, and made his way to an isolated spot near the kitchen. A large plastic garbage disposal unit sat in a hallway outside the cafeteria. When it was full, it would be rolled outside and hauled away by the trash company. Before entering the hallway, he removed a small device from his pocket and switched on the power. It would temporarily jam the signals of any nearby security cameras. He could not risk being caught on camera.

On his way to Miami, Dr. Catalyst had stopped at a hardware store and purchased a few supplies. Now, hidden from view, he duct-taped an emergency road flare to a plastic bottle of lighter fluid. He pushed the garbage unit down the hallway, until it stood directly beneath an air-conditioning vent that fed into the hospital's main ventilation system.

It was now or never. Dr. Catalyst struck the flare head against the wall, and it burst into a bright, hissing flame. He tossed the burning bundle inside the garbage unit. The flare would burn down like a candle and the heat would eventually melt the plastic bottle, igniting the lighter fluid inside. Most of the garbage in the bin was plastic and paper, and would only produce smoke. But it would be enough to set off the alarm.

Dr. Catalyst walked away, returning to the lobby and exiting the building. A few minutes later he pulled his police cruiser in front of the hospital and waited. He rolled the window down on the passenger side of the car and was soon rewarded by the shrieking fire alarm.

Soon the evacuation began. Patients who could walk exited first, escorted by orderlies and nurses. Then came others, being pushed on gurneys and rolling hospital beds. Smoke filtered out of the ventilation system on the roof. The evacuation continued. Dr. Catalyst scanned the crowd, watching for his quarry.

His patience paid off. Emmet and Calvin left the lobby, wearing bewildered expressions.

Dr. Catalyst exited the police car and made his way through the crowd toward them. The nameplate above the badge on his uniform said FULMAN.

Now came the hard part. The area in front of the hospital was teeming with people. He would need to be very careful and hope the boys didn't recognize him from the school. All he needed was a few minutes. Just a little luck, and he would have his revenge.

He worked his way through the crowd until he was in front of the boys.

"Hey, guys," he said, a friendly tone in his voice. "Are you by any chance Emmet Doyle and Calvin Geaux?"

"Yeah," Emmet said, with a wary look on his face.

"Officer Stukaczowski just radioed ahead. I'm Officer Fulman. Your parents are going to be moved to Miami General, because of the fire. He wants to meet us there. Asked me to transport you." Dr. Catalyst didn't wait for an answer. If you acted like you were in charge, most people would follow along. So he turned and started walking back toward the cruiser.

With a quick glance over his shoulder, he found Emmet and Calvin were following him.

His plan was working to perfection.

15

EMMET AND CALVIN FOLLOWED THE POLICE OFFICER through the chaotic crowd in front of the hospital. There was an obstacle course of wheelchairs, hospital beds, and ambulances to maneuver through before they finally reached the curb where the cruiser was parked.

Fire trucks were starting to arrive, which only added to the noise and confusion. As firefighters jumped off the trucks, the space in front of the hospital grew more crowded. Additional ambulances and paramedics were arriving by the second. Emmet and Calvin had a hard time keeping up with the policeman in all the confusion.

Something was still nagging at Emmet, though. Everything felt off-kilter. He couldn't tell what it was that bothered him. Maybe he was just all jangled up. After all, it wasn't every week that he was attacked by a giant ball of claws and teeth. More like every other.

"Doesn't this seem a little odd to you?" Emmet said quietly to Calvin.

"What?"

Officer Fulman was a few feet ahead of them, dodging through the crowd. Every so often he glanced over his shoulder to make sure they were following along.

"All of this. First, that monster cat attacks us. A few hours later we're in the hospital, and while everyone is in surgery a fire breaks out?"

"Fires happen sometimes. Even in hospitals," Calvin said.

Emmet sighed. *Thank you, Captain Obvious.*

Then he felt guilty. Calvin was probably worried about his mom and uncle. It was natural to be preoccupied.

But Emmet didn't like this. And he didn't like how quickly this Officer Fulman had led them away from the crowd.

Calvin wouldn't naturally suspect someone in authority of being up to no good. Officer Fulman was a law-and-order guy, with the uniform and everything. But ever since Emmet moved to Florida and met a couple of giant Pterogators on his first day, he had grown to suspect everyone.

"Have you ever seen this cop before?" he asked.

"No. Why?"

"I just wondered why Stuke's dad would send someone unfamiliar, if he couldn't come himself," Emmet said.

Calvin shrugged. "Just because we don't recognize him doesn't mean he isn't legit. Florida City has a lot of police officers. Heck, there are even people on the task force we haven't met." Calvin always shrugged. It was his natural reaction to Emmet's conspiracy theories.

The cop looked over his shoulder, and for just a brief moment, Emmet saw something flash through his eyes before he spoke. It wasn't concern. Or even politeness. It was anger. It was only there for a second. Emmet tried telling himself he was being paranoid, but he knew he wasn't. Officer Fulman had looked at him with hate in his eyes.

"Hurry up, fellas. I need to get you out of here," Fulman said.

Warning bells were going off in Emmet's head like crazy. He looked around for another police officer. Right at that moment, they all seemed to be inside with the firefighters, helping to evacuate the patients. Officer Fulman reached the back door of his car and opened it, standing aside for Emmet and Calvin to get in. He smiled, but his face was all stiff and wrong. It was the fakest smile Emmet had ever seen.

"Did you say Sergeant Stukaczowski wanted you to take us to Miami General?" Emmet asked, trying to sound as nonchalant as he could.

"That's right," he said. "And we need to hurry." He took the radio microphone from his shoulder. "Unit three-six-five, show me inbound," he said into the mic. Emmet didn't wait for the dispatcher or anyone else to respond to his radio call. Because there was no Sergeant Stukaczowski. Stuke's dad was a lieutenant.

"Calvin, run!" he said, shoving his friend away from the police car. Calvin's face was a mask of surprise and confusion. He nearly stumbled over an elderly patient who was being pushed in a wheelchair on the sidewalk. The police officer — Emmet was now certain it was Dr. Catalyst, or someone helping him — froze for a moment. "You boys! Quit messing around. We need —"

"Help!" Emmet shouted "It's Dr. Catalyst! Help! Help!"

"What?" Calvin said, still momentarily confused.

"Run, Calvin! Get help!" Emmet shouted.

Dr. Catalyst started toward Emmet, who was backing up and still shouting. They were starting to attract attention over the noise and confusion. A few nurses and orderlies stopped what they were doing to gawk.

"I'm taking you boys in!" Dr. Catalyst called. "Police matter! Everyone step back!" He continued to advance.

Calvin looked unsure of what to do, standing between the face of authority and his shouting friend. Dr.

Catalyst must have decided he'd be an easier catch. He turned and lunged at Calvin.

"NO!" Emmet shouted. "Calvin! Run!" Calvin finally seemed to snap out of his stupor. He darted around the wheelchair, with Dr. Catalyst in pursuit.

"What's going on here?" a burly orderly asked Emmet. He had a thick beard and glasses, and looked like he could handle himself.

"That's not a real cop! It's Dr. Catalyst! He's trying to kidnap my friend!"

"Yeah, sure, kid," he said. "What'd you do? Steal something?"

"No! My dad is in sur —" He stopped. Dr. Catalyst was closing in on Calvin. The crowd in front of the hospital made escape too difficult.

"Get a cop! A real one!" Emmet shouted at the orderly as he took off after them.

There was plenty of light outside from the hospital, streetlights, and all the emergency vehicles, but Emmet still couldn't spot any police officers. The parking lot was packed with people, like a river of human beings was flooding out of the doors. Calvin's instincts had told him to run back inside to safety, but he was running against the onslaught of people who were evacuating. Dr. Catalyst was closing in. Emmet sprinted hard after them. He had to yell really loudly to be heard over the din.

"Hey! Fake cop who's really Dr. Catalyst! Isn't it me you want? Emmet Doyle? Your archnemesis?"

Somehow, over all the noise, Dr. Catalyst had heard him. Emmet waited until he saw Calvin dart out of sight into the mass of people. At least he would be safe and could summon help. Dr. Catalyst looked at Emmet, then back at where Calvin had disappeared. He didn't hesitate.

"Somebody stop that kid!" he shouted, pointing at Emmet.

"Come and get me!" Emmet yelled back.

He turned and ran as fast as he could.

Away from the hospital and into the dark Miami streets.

16

SINCE EMMET LIVED IN FLORIDA CITY, HE HAD ONLY been able to come to Miami a couple of times to visit Stuke in the hospital. Now, running blindly into the city, Emmet realized he had no idea where he was. He only knew there were two directions he could go: forward, or back toward his pursuer. He should have run around the side of the building and gone in another entrance. Once there it would have made sense to find a police officer, a real one, and have them get Lieutenant Stukaczowski on the radio.

But Dr. Catalyst had been there, right there, dressed like a police officer and about to grab Emmet's best friend. Calvin had saved Emmet more times than he could count, and in that moment, drawing the madman away from his friend was the only thing Emmet could think to do.

He knew Dr. Catalyst hated his dad and Dr. Geaux. He probably hated Uncle Yaha, and maybe even Calvin, despite him being his grandson. But if there was one person the crazed scientist really hated, it was Emmet himself.

The feeling was mutual.

Calvin had made it back into the hospital, Emmet was sure of it. Calvin was calm and respectful. He was the kind of kid a police officer was likely to believe if they said something was amiss. That would come in handy when he was trying to explain what was going on, while Dr. Catalyst chased Emmet.

Emmet scanned the streets as he ran, searching for his best escape route. The very heavily traveled South Dixie Highway bordered South Miami Hospital to the east and south. Running toward the highway was not an option. Emmet had no desire to escape Dr. Catalyst's clutches only to be flattened by a semitruck. The hospital's main entrance was on 73rd Street, so he ran along the sidewalk. He glanced over his shoulder and didn't see Dr. Catalyst coming after him. Maybe he was taking a different route and trying to cut him off somehow. Or maybe he'd given up. . . .

Emmet couldn't take the chance. He kept running up the street until he came to the first intersection. With a fifty-fifty shot, he turned left. Now he was running along Sunset Drive. As he ran, Emmet clutched at his pockets, looking for his cell phone. He realized with a pang of dread that he'd left it at Calvin's house amidst all the confusion. Emmet cursed his luck. Sometimes, when you're attacked by a giant furry ball of rage and have to rush off with your dad in an ambulance, you forget stuff.

Emmet ran on, hoping to see someone walking by, or an open storefront, anyone to call the police. But it was too late in the night. He tried flagging down a couple of cars, but no one stopped.

It was no good being out in the open like this. Dr. Catalyst could be anywhere.

A police car came screaming up 73rd Street, screeching to a halt at the Sunset intersection. Its lights were flashing and the sirens were running. Emmet wanted to believe this was a real cop, but something told him he wasn't that lucky. He tried to hide by cutting to his left, lunging off the sidewalk and into the shadows.

But he wasn't quick enough. Dr. Catalyst must have spotted Emmet because the car turned onto the street, speeding after him. But the madman didn't think like a real cop. This stretch of Sunset was a wide boulevard, separated in the center by a tree-lined median. He had to pull over to the far side of it to travel in the right direction. There was a grassy divider between them now, which gave Emmet a temporary bit of extra time.

He was really sprinting now. His legs burned. He came to another intersection and faked like he would keep running along Sunset, then quickly cut down the side street. The move caught his pursuer by surprise. He had to accelerate farther down the street, until there was a spot where he could cross the boulevard and zoom back in Emmet's direction.

Emmet frantically searched his surroundings. He'd entered a residential street. He thought about trying to knock on one of the doors for help, but decided that yelling and screaming "Call 9-1-1!" might seem suspect if there was already a cop car chasing him. By the time he got a chance to explain, Dr. Catalyst would be right there, hand on Emmet's shoulder, feeding the home-owner some line about delinquent kids. Emmet had to find a place to hide. A place to lose him.

Up ahead, Emmet spied the lighted parking lot of an elementary school. Schools were locked up at night, but they had playgrounds. This was his chance to get off the street. It would be dark and would take away the advantage of the car. Emmet could outrun Dr. Catalyst until Calvin brought the cops. Or called the Marines. Or however he chose to get Emmet out of this mess. Hopefully the Marines.

The cop car was turning onto the street just as Emmet reached the elementary school. He ran across the parking lot, where he discovered the tiny flaw in his plan. The street and parking lot were well lit. The playground was not. It was shrouded in shadows behind the school. Good for hiding, but not good for seeing where he was going.

The sound of the siren drew closer. Emmet sped around the corner of the building and sprinted for the farthest, darkest corner of the playground. The cruiser screeched to a halt in the parking lot. Then a car door slammed.

Dr. Catalyst was coming.

Come on, Calvin, Emmet thought. *Where's my backup?*

He kept running, dodging the dim shapes of jungle gyms and merry-go-rounds, risking a look over his shoulder to try and catch sight of his pursuer. All Emmet saw was a bouncing flashlight beam coming from the direction of the parking lot. Dr. Catalyst would turn the corner any second. If Emmet didn't find a place to hide, he'd be toast.

That's when he ran face-first into a tetherball pole. It knocked Emmet flat on his back. The last thing he remembered was seeing stars. He couldn't tell if they were the stars up in the night sky or the kind you see when you smack your head up against a piece of iron.

It didn't really matter, because after that one final thought, Emmet didn't see or remember anything at all.

17

FOR ONE OF THE FEW TIMES IN HIS LIFE, CALVIN GEAUX
defied the rules. As he darted through the crowd,
dozens of hospital personnel yelled at him to turn
around and go the other way. He just put his head down
and kept going. Once inside the lobby, he found it was
even more chaotic than outside. Some of the patients
being evacuated were no doubt seriously ill or injured.
It was a carefully coordinated dance to get everyone
out as quickly and as safely as possible.

Just past the information desk, Calvin spied a police
officer helping an orderly push a large, heavy gurney.

"Officer! I need to report a crime!" Calvin said.

"Kind of busy right now, kid," the officer replied.

"It's Dr. Catalyst! He's here at the hospital. My name is Calvin Geaux, my mom is —"

The police officer was actually a Dade County sheriff's deputy. His nameplate said SGT. J. D. ARTH. He was medium height, his black hair lined with streaks of gray. And he was concentrating on the task at hand — not paying attention to Calvin.

"Catalyst? You mean that joker from down in the Glades? The one that's been all over the news? What would he be doing at South Miami Hospital?" The officer never looked at Calvin as he spoke, his attention focused on the crowd and the patient he was assisting.

"Right now he's trying to kidnap my friend Emmet. Look, my mom is Dr. Geaux. Dr. Rosalita Geaux. She's the head of the governor's Dr. Catalyst task force. She's in surgery. We were attacked by one of Dr. Catalyst's newest genetically enhanced creatures tonight."

"Listen, kid, we've got an emergency here. Why don't you call it in and if we can get a spare person down here we'll take your statement, and —"

Calvin didn't wait for him to finish. He dodged through and around another group of evacuating patients and dashed toward the elevators. Now he was certain Dr. Catalyst was behind the fire. It was the perfect cover.

"Hey, kid!" the deputy shouted. "Get back here; you need to get out!"

All Calvin could think to do was to make his way back to the OR waiting room to find Nurse Hernandez, if he could. She would believe him, and at least find help. Emmet didn't have much time. Dr. Catalyst had planned this perfectly. No matter how convincing Emmet was, he'd never get anyone to believe that he wasn't just trying to evade the police.

There were two orderlies watching the elevators, making sure they were being used exclusively for patients who could not walk. Calvin tried to get on one when the door opened, but one of the orderlies put out his hand.

"No way, kid. Patients only on the elevators. You need to exit the hospital."

Calvin was beyond the point of listening to the authorities. Instead of leaving as he'd been instructed, he raced to the nearby stairway. It was also crowded with a crush of descending patients and staff. Calvin dodged his way through and around them as he made his way up toward the OR waiting room. It took him much longer than he'd hoped, and with each second ticking by, he grew more worried about Emmet. He finally reached the floor and burst into the hallway, running to the waiting room.

It was empty.

He wondered if perhaps they had already evacuated his mom, Uncle Yaha, and Dr. Doyle because they were high-priority patients. There might not be anyone here to help him. The alarm was still blaring loudly, giving him a headache.

There was a desk in the corner of the waiting room, and behind it were doors leading to the surgical units. Calvin approached the desk. Each door had a small window in it, but he saw no one moving about. And he certainly couldn't hear anyone.

"Hello?" he shouted as loud as he could. His voice was drowned out by the alarm.

"Calvin?"

He jumped and spun around to find Lieutenant Stukaczowski standing there.

"Oh, geez," Calvin said, suddenly realizing how out of breath he was. He'd been running on adrenaline the whole time. Now that Stuke's dad was here, he felt an enormous sense of relief. But they still had to find Emmet.

"Where's Emmet, Calvin?"

"He . . . There was a fire. We had to leave. The nurse said they would transport our parents to another hospital. And then when we got outside, there was a policeman, and he said you had radioed ahead for him to take us to the hospital because of the fire. Emmet thought something was wrong, and then right before we got in the car, Emmet asked him if Sergeant Stukaczowski really wanted us to leave before he got here. And the cop said yes. That's when Emmet must have known he was a fake cop, because you're a lieutenant."

"That Emmet is a smart kid. Was it the same guy you saw in the school?"

"I don't know. He had blond hair instead of black and a mustache. But he could have been wearing a disguise, I guess."

"What kind of uniform was he wearing? What did the car look like?"

"It was a Florida City uniform. The car said Florida City, but that's all I know."

"Where is Emmet now?"

"That's just it. I tried to run back into the hospital for help. The cop . . . Dr. Catalyst was chasing me. With all the people rushing out, I was having a hard time getting in. He was closing in on me, when Emmet smarted off at him and made him stop for a second. It gave me enough time to get into the crowd and get away. But I think he took off after Emmet."

"Okay," Lieutenant Stukaczowski said. "You did really well. Right now, my wife, my son, Riley, and Raeburn are waiting in the car downstairs. Your parents have been transported to Miami General."

"But what about Emmet?"

"We're going to find him. My guess is Emmet is still on foot and somewhere in the area. But if Dr. Catalyst is using a real FCPD car, it will have a transponder in it. We'll be able to track him. Even if he managed to catch Emmet, we can follow them."

"But what if he's using a fake car?" Calvin asked.

"We're going to set up a perimeter with roadblocks. I'm betting on Emmet. I'm betting he's stayed away from Dr. Catalyst long enough for you to get help."

"You have to find him, Lieutenant Stukaczowski. This is all my fault. All of it. And now . . . even when . . . he knew it was my fault, he still tried to save my life." For the first time he could remember in a long time, Calvin felt tears forming in his eyes.

"Calvin, you listen to me. This is not your fault. None of it. Most of what we know about this creep we got from the two of you. You're two of the most amazing kids I've ever seen. So stop blaming yourself." He put his arm around Calvin's shoulders. "Now come on, we've got to get you to your parents, and I've got a perp to catch."

"You've got to find Emmet, sir. You've got to."

"Don't worry, Calvin. We will," he said.

As they headed back down the stairs, Lieutenant Stukaczowski pulled his cell phone from his pocket and started issuing orders.

The manhunt was on.

18

EMMET WOKE UP WHEN THE CAR HE WAS RIDING IN jolted over a big rut in the road. It was still dark. His face hurt. It hurt a lot. His vision was blurry. He would have tried to touch his face to find out what was wrong with his eyes, but his hands were restrained somehow. He thought one of his eyes might be swollen shut.

As he slowly came to, Emmet realized he was lying in the backseat of a car. Another big jolt in the road both hurt and further brought him awake. Emmet rose up, peering out of the one eye that he could open all the way. He was in a police car. There was a cage between himself and the driver.

"Dr. Catalyst, I presume?" Emmet said. He tasted a little blood in his mouth. He must have split his lip when he collided with the pole. "I've always wanted to say that. Once you were caught."

There was just enough illumination from the dashboard to see the driver's dark eyes glare at Emmet from the rearview mirror. Then he laughed. It was kind of a snort, really.

"I'm not the one who's caught." He sneered at Emmet.

"It's only a matter of time, Doc. Is it okay if I call you Doc? It's a lot less formal. And Dr. Catalyst . . . well, as villain names go, you could have done better. You should have went with Extremo, or Nut-Job-a-Tron, or something. Most people think a *catalyst* is a house cat. Like a tabby or a calico."

"Shut up," Dr. Catalyst spat. "Just shut your mouth."

"Why? What are you going to do? Stop the car? Teach me a lesson? I just thought we might as well get to know each other. Before the cops get here."

"The cops aren't coming," he said.

"Geez, you really aren't very bright are you? Ever since you kidnapped my dad, I've been wearing a tracker. So has Calvin and everyone on the task force." Emmet looked out the window. "Probably a helicopter following us right now." He was lying. He was supposed to keep his cell phone with him at all times. It could be tracked. He had screwed up, leaving it at Calvin's house.

Dr. Catalyst stared at Emmet in the rearview mirror. Emmet could tell from his smug expression that the man sensed he was lying.

"You're not wearing a tracker. I swept you for any device and there was nothing on you. I have tech better than anything the task force has. You're clean. Now shut up."

"So tell me, Dr. Cat Litter, what's the endgame here? Going to drug me and put me in a cage like you did with my dad? Give me a couple of Pterogators as prison guards? That really worked out well, didn't it? How is your arm, by the way? 'Cause when that beast of yours took a bite . . . wow . . . I'll bet that stung. In case you haven't figured it out yet, you're a really lousy kidnapper. I mean, you couldn't even hold on to my dog. Some genius environmentalist whacko you are." As Emmet talked, he kept looking out the windows, hoping he could figure out where they were. The road was definitely not blacktop. He heard gravel pinging against the bottom of the car, and there were trees and bushes close to the road. They were in the middle of nowhere.

"Oh, there won't be any prolonged kidnapping this time. In fact, I'm going to give you a chance to escape. All you have to do is pass a little test. The instructor who is running it has a particular interest in you. Well, actually, it's more an interest in how the meat on your bones tastes. I believe you've already met your instructor. A couple of times this week, in fact?"

Emmet had to admit that made him a little nervous. The face of the creature that had now twice attacked him, its mouth full of razor-sharp teeth, flashed in his memory. For a second, Emmet was overcome by a fearful shudder that ran through him.

He had to keep Dr. Catalyst off his game. The angrier he could make Dr. Catalyst — the longer he could keep him talking — the more likely it was that the loon would slip up and reveal something about where they were going. It could give Emmet a clue about which direction to take when he escaped. If he escaped.

No. When he escaped. *Think positive,* Emmet told himself. *Calvin has the cavalry on the way.*

"I'm sorry, what were you saying?" Emmet said. "I dozed off a little at the beginning there. Something about a test? Speaking of . . . that reminds me, I've got an algebra test this week. I should study for that if we're going to be gone for a while. You wouldn't mind making a quick stop to pick up my homework, would you?"

Dr. Catalyst didn't answer. They kept driving down the rutted road. Each bump sent Emmet bouncing in the seat. The farther they went, the more disheartened Emmet became. Wherever this place was, it had to be way off the grid.

"Geez," Emmet said. "Two words: *shock absorbers.*"

Still nothing.

"So back to this plan of yours," Emmet said. "What have you got? I mean, you've screwed up everything else so far. The park service has captured almost all of the Pterogators. From what I hear, the Muraecudas haven't been seen in weeks, and the Blood Jackets are dropping out of the sky. All you've done is make everything worse —"

"Keep talking," Dr. Catalyst snapped. "Once you're alone with my newest creation you'll see just how much worse it can get. If I'm lucky, the first thing the Swamp Cat bites off is your smart mouth."

"Ha, good one!" Emmet said. But in truth he looked out the window and winced. He'd already met this new creation, and it had nearly clawed three fully grown adults to death in a matter of moments. The idea of getting up close and personal with this "Swamp Cat" again terrified Emmet.

The car slowed down, and they turned off the road onto an even more narrow lane. A few yards in, an automatic gate opened, and they pulled up to a large barn. A door on the barn rose, and Dr. Catalyst pulled the car inside.

"We're here. I'm going to bring you out and lock you up. Don't bother trying anything. There's no one anywhere nearby that can help you. No one even knows where this place is."

Emmet didn't say anything as Dr. Catalyst climbed out of the car and opened the back door. Emmet sat still and made the man reach inside to pull him out. Dr. Catalyst had wrapped plastic flex-cuffs on Emmet's hands, and they were now digging into his wrists.

"What's the matter?" Dr. Catalyst asked. "No snappy comeback? No insulting comments? No witty one-liners? Has the 'cat' got your tongue, Emmet? If it doesn't now, it will soon enough. And the rest of you, too."

He shoved Emmet toward a door.

"Isn't that funny. All your bravado. Your smart mouth. Now you've got nothing to say?" Dr. Catalyst was gloating now. Time to put an end to that.

"Oh, I've got something to say, all right," Emmet said as Dr. Catalyst opened the door and shoved him into a small, windowless room. He stood in the doorway, glaring at Emmet.

"And what is that?" Dr. Catalyst said.

Emmet stared back at him, doing his best not to appear scared or nervous.

"Whatever it is you're going to do? Just get on with it. I'm bored."

Dr. Catalyst smirked and slammed the door. Then Emmet heard the door lock shut.

He was trapped.

19

AS THE HOURS PASSED, CALVIN GREW MORE WORRIED. Lieutenant Stukaczowski had gone ahead with his roadblocks. With the assistance of the Dade County sheriff's department, he had searched every inch of the blocks surrounding the hospital. They had failed to turn up Emmet. Calvin couldn't explain why, but he felt that they were too late.

Lieutenant Stukaczowski suggested that since Dr. Catalyst had dressed as a police officer, and it was still dark, Emmet was staying hidden. When the morning light broke, and Emmet could see clearly, he'd come out of hiding.

But Calvin didn't believe it. In his bones, he felt Dr. Catalyst had Emmet. His friend hadn't been able to escape.

The OR waiting room at Miami General Hospital was a lot like its counterpart at South Miami. It was full of uncomfortable chairs, old magazines, and worn carpet. Stuke's mom had taken Riley, Raeburn, and Stuke down to the cafeteria to get something to eat. It was past midnight now, and Calvin wasn't hungry. He was too nervous to eat. He had to find Emmet. For some reason he felt like he was the only one who could.

Calvin started thinking about the Everglades, picturing the massive River of Grass in his mind. When his mom told people that Calvin was the best Everglades guide under eighteen around, she wasn't just bragging. He knew the swamp as well as anyone could. He tried to think of a place Dr. Catalyst could keep his new creature a secret. It would need to be a spot with solid ground. Wild cats, even feral house cats, were hunters. There were Florida panthers in the swamp, but they needed solid ground to catch the deer and other creatures they hunted. They couldn't chase prey through the water or swampy marshland.

So it would be a place with dry ground, but that remained accessible to the Everglades. There were potentially hundreds of locations like that. Calvin needed to narrow the scope. Emmet didn't have much time, if any. There was only one person Calvin could think of who might know where to search.

His uncle Yaha.

Who right now was lying in intensive care, unconscious and unable to talk.

If Uncle Yaha had treated Dr. Catalyst's wounds after the Pterogator bite, perhaps he'd told Yaha something about where he was living and working in the Everglades. It was the only thing Calvin could think of that might help. The question was, how would he get to Yaha, to ask him? And would Yaha even be able to answer those questions?

Calvin thought some more about it. Then he had an idea.

This OR waiting room had a front desk, much like the one at South Miami, but here it was staffed by an elderly lady in a white coat. She was probably a volunteer. Calvin walked slowly up to her.

"Can I help you, young man?" She had silver-gray hair and kind of reminded him of Mrs. Clawson a little bit.

"I need to see my great-uncle; his name is Yaha. He's in intensive care," Calvin said.

She nodded and tapped a keyboard for a few seconds.

"I'm very sorry, young man," she said. "But according to my screen, your uncle cannot see anyone yet. He's still unconscious."

"I know, but he's a . . . we're a . . . my uncle and I are Seminoles. He needs to be given a special prayer. It's a tradition in our tribe when someone is sick. Don't you have to let him have his religious . . . needs . . . and things . . . given to him?" Calvin tried to look serious, but he was a horrible liar. If Emmet were here, they would already be inside, getting the information out of Yaha somehow.

The lady sat back in her chair. It was clear he had caught her by surprise.

"Well, yes, there is a hospital policy for that, but usually we have a priest or someone —"

"I can say the prayer. I've been through the ceremony many times." Calvin looked at her with sad eyes. "So many times. My family is very sick."

"Oh, I'm so sorry. Uh. You can . . . I don't . . . we don't allow anyone under sixteen in the intensive care unit without an adult present."

"I understand. But Seminole boys go through a ceremony at my age and are considered men." Calvin was starting to get the hang of lying. He had to do it to save his friend. It got easier the more you did it. "So you have to recognize me according to our treaty with the United States government."

Calvin felt horrible, because the kind lady's face was growing more confused and alarmed as he talked.

"As an adult member of a sovereign nation, you have to let me in to say the prayer. If something happens and my uncle passes, he will not be able to cross over to the spirit world. You wouldn't want to be responsible for that, would you?" Calvin tried to keep his hands from shaking. He was certain she would see right through the tall tale he was spinning.

"I . . . No, of course not." The lady leaned forward in her chair and reached for the phone. "I'm going to have to check ——"

"Ma'am," Calvin interrupted her. "We don't have much time. My uncle was gravely wounded. He might not make it. I need to see him. Or I'll bring shame on my family."

The lady got a confused and worried look on her face. Calvin tried to keep a somber expression on his face, but on the inside he was shaking like a leaf. He felt horrible for deceiving the poor woman.

"All right," she said. "I'll take you back. But you can't take very long. It's not allowed. And . . ."

"I'll be quick," he promised.

The lady stood and waved him around he desk.

"Follow me," she said.

Calvin did.

20

THE ROOM WAS ABOUT TEN FEET BY TEN FEET, WITH A single low-wattage lightbulb hanging from the ceiling. With his hands still bound behind him, Emmet searched over every inch of the room. It was constructed of plain, unpainted drywall, built and framed in an open space of the old barn. Maybe Dr. Catalyst had planned to use it as an office at some point.

On the drive here, he told Emmet that he had to pass a test. The instructor was going to be the Swamp Cat. Emmet didn't care for the sound of that one bit. There was no telling what Dr. Catalyst had in store for him. Hopefully it didn't involve opening the door to the room he was in and shoving the Swamp Cat inside. That wouldn't end well.

Emmet sauntered over to the door and turned his back to it, trying the knob with his bound hands, just to make sure it was locked. It was, but you never knew. If he'd sat against the far wall and the door had been unlocked the whole time, he would have felt pretty foolish.

Emmet walked the perimeter of the room one more time. The light was so dim it made it nearly impossible to see anything, but he looked all the same. There was no way to reach the roof that he could find. He checked the drywall in the corners and thought about trying to kick his way through, but that would make a lot of noise. No doubt Dr. Catalyst would frown on escape attempts before the "test" had begun.

A strange odor reached Emmet's nose. It smelled like . . . he wasn't sure exactly . . . maybe like an animal. Which made sense, what with him being trapped in a barn. But he had lived in Montana and been around horses and cattle. This smell wasn't like a barn animal.

From someplace close by came the uncanny roar of the Swamp Cat. It was so sudden and unexpected that Emmet yelped in surprise, the two noises echoing together in the barn. The creature roared again and again, whipping itself into a frenzy. Try as he might to keep focused on escaping, the continuous caterwauling of the beast was unsettling.

"Do you hear that?" Dr. Catalyst's voice came through

the door. Emmet wasn't expecting him and he involuntarily jumped.

"Your instructor has arrived and he is quite anxious to begin the test," he said. "He has been created especially for you, Emmet Doyle. I took the time and expense away from my crusade to save the Everglades, to create a hybrid specifically for hunting you down. You should feel honored."

Emmet didn't say anything — A) because Dr. Catalyst was crazy, and B) because he was terrified. But he was determined not to let the creep know it.

"What's the matter, Emmet?" Dr. Catalyst crowed from behind the door. "Where's your smart mouth now? Nothing to say?"

"I'm sorry, were you talking to me?" Emmet said. "I was actually busy playing Hacky Sack and you interrupted me. I was up to thirty-seven. That's a personal record. Hacky Sack is a lot harder than it looks."

Now it was Dr. Catalyst's turn to not say anything. He probably wasn't used to dealing with smart-alecky twelve-year-old kids. Despite all of his little manifestos and press releases and videos he sent to the media claiming to be this crusader saving the environment, he wasn't any of that. He was a terrorist, a bully, and a criminal. He didn't know what to do when people didn't fear him. Which isn't to say that Emmet didn't fear him, because he did. But he'd let the Swamp Cat eat him before he'd give an inch to this loser.

"By the way, if I have to take a test," Emmet said, "give that *creation* of yours a bath, will ya? It stinks to high heaven. I like a clean work environment, not instructors who smell like rotten meat. Makes it easier to concentrate."

"Go ahead. Crack all the stupid jokes you want," Dr. Catalyst said. "You don't fool me. You're petrified."

"Oh, really? Are you so sure about that, Dr. C? Or should I say Grandpa Geaux?"

Even through the door, Emmet could hear the sharp intake of breath.

"What did you say?"

"That's right, Gramps. When Calvin and I got home from school today, there was somebody waiting for us. I believe you know him as Yaha? He's a doctor, right? Fixed up your arm after the Pterogator bit it? *Anyhoo*, he told us the whole story. Well, not the whole story, because you sent in your smelly little beast and that screwed things up a bit. But we got enough. And unfortunately for you, you caught me instead of Calvin. You see, Calvin's the smart one. I'm just here for comic relief. He recognized you in the school when you came in during the Blood Jacket att —"

"*Shut up!*" Dr. Catalyst screamed, interrupting him.

"Shut your mouth! You don't know anything!" His voice was strained. Now he was really agitated.

"You do know it's rude for a host to interrupt his guests, right?" Emmet said. "Like I was saying, by now Calvin has revealed your real identity to the police. They'll be combing the Glades for this place. I'll bet your picture is on every news station and website there is in the entire state. The jig, as they say, is up. Gramps."

Emmet stepped back from the door and peered at the base of it. There was a tiny space between the door and the floor. He could still see the shadows of Dr. Catalyst's feet. They remained there, totally still. Emmet decided to poke the bear a little more.

"By the way, trying to kill your own grandson? I mean, that's not very grandfatherly. What did Calvin ever do to you? Not only are you horrible at being an ecoterrorist, you're really bad at the whole grandfathering thing. I'd be happy to give you a few pointers. My grandpa Doyle takes me fishing and sends me presents. Let me think . . . Nope, he's never once tried to kill me with a genetically altered super-predator, or kidnapped my best friend's dad."

"You know nothing about me *or* my family," Dr. Catalyst spat. "Nothing. Stay in there and keep your mouth shut. At dawn, the test begins."

"I don't think you have that much time," Emmet said.

"What could possibly make you think that?"

"The task force knows who you are. And they're really smart, tough people. Despite all of your impressive gizmos and technology, they have *more* technology and even *better* gizmos. And Lieutenant Stukaczowski is in charge now. Remember when you sicced the Muraecudas on us? The kid who got all chewed up was his son. I think if he gets his hands on you, he'll crack your head open like a peanut. Actually, since he's not a total whackjob like you, he'll probably just slap the cuffs on you. Although the whole peanut scenario would be really fun to see."

"Whatever happens to me, Doyle, they'll never find you in time."

"Sure they will. Right now they've got people looking at property records, bank accounts, security camera footage, and anything else you might have even breathed on. They'll be here soon. And besides that, I know something you don't."

"And what would that be?"

"Calvin is coming for me," Emmet said.

"He doesn't know where you are, either. I'll give you credit for being a tough kid. But you're dreaming."

"Am I, Grandpa Geaux? You don't even know your own grandson. I wouldn't underestimate him if I were you. He knows the Everglades. I'll bet he's on his way here right now."

Dr. Catalyst let out a single loud laugh. "Oh, I'll take that bet. You have until dawn."

"Dawn? Great. That will give me plenty of time to break my personal Hacky Sack record. Why don't you go off and do some supervillain stuff so I can practice? Check the news while you're at it. You might see your picture. It's kind of cool to see yourself on TV."

Emmet glanced down at the bottom of the door. The shadows had disappeared. Dr. Catalyst must have stormed off to get ready for Emmet's test, whatever it was going to be. Or else he had sufficiently angered him.

Emmet strolled around the perimeter of the room one more time looking for something, anything that might lead to a way out. A weak spot in the wall. A vent or tool that he could use to pry the door open. He knew the chances of getting out were remote, but he had to try.

When he had all but given up hope, Emmet finally spied a nail sticking out of the drywall near the back corner. That was interesting. He turned around, feeling over the wall with his bound hands, until his finger scraped against the warm metal. It stuck out about a half inch. Emmet grabbed and pulled at it, but it was hard to get a grip with his hands cuffed behind him. Pulling and straining until sweat was pouring down his face, he managed to unplug the nail another half inch. The muscles in his shoulders and arms were cramping from the stress. He leaned against the wall to rest a bit. He had an idea.

Emmet lay down on the floor and put his feet up on the wall, squeezing the nail head between the thick rubber heels of his sneakers. He flexed his legs, pushing his toes forward and his heels up, almost as if the wall were the floor and he was trying to stand on the tips of his toes. Nothing happened.

He gathered himself and tried again. It was important to try to stay quiet, in case Dr. Catalyst heard him. But he was breathing heavily and grunting with the strain. Still, nothing was happening.

Emmet flexed as hard as he could one more time. When he felt the nail give a little he nearly shouted in a delirious burst of happiness. Biting his lip, he kept yanking at it with his heels, pulling more and more of it free from the wall. Then he scrambled upright and reached back with his hands to grab it. Twisting and turning, Emmet managed to loosen it until it finally popped free. Feeling around with his hands, he figured it was probably four inches long.

He slipped it into the back pocket of his jeans.

A nail. It wasn't much. But it was something.

21

THE LADY FROM THE INFORMATION DESK ESCORTED Calvin through the doors and into the intensive care unit. He got a few curious stares from nurses and aides, but walking beside hospital staff must have validated his presence there. She led him down a corridor and around a corner to a room. Looking through the window, Calvin could see his uncle Yaha lying in a hospital bed. Lots of wires and tubes were hooked up to him.

"Here you go, young man," the lady said. "You'll need to be quick and try not to disturb him. Once you're done, please come straight back to the waiting room."

"I will, ma'am," Calvin said politely. "Thank you."

She left him in the hallway, the rubber soles of her shoes squeaking on the tile floor as she walked away. Calvin took a deep breath and pushed open the heavy door, walking quickly to his uncle's bedside.

Calvin was always surprised by how noisy a hospital room was. Monitors beeped and machines whirred. His uncle's labored breathing could barely be heard over the sound of the equipment. The old man's head sank into the pillow, an oxygen tube attached to his nose. An IV bag was dripping medicine slowly into a tube inserted into his arm at the elbow.

Calvin pulled back the sheet until he found his uncle's hand beneath it. Carefully he gripped it. The older man didn't move, or give any indication that he was aware of his surroundings.

"Uncle Yaha. It's me, Calvin. Can you hear me? If you can hear me, please squeeze my hand." Calvin waited. Nothing happened.

"Please, Uncle. *Please* hear me. I need your help. Grandfather has taken my friend Emmet. Emmet is in danger. Grandfather has lost his way. I need you to help me find him. So I can bring him back to the right path. Please squeeze my hand if you understand." Calvin waited. Each second ticking by seemed like an eternity. Still his uncle did not respond. Calvin didn't know what else to do.

He didn't believe that Lieutenant Stukaczowski and the rest of the task force would find Emmet in time. This had been his only shot, the one thing he could think of that might give Emmet a fighting chance. He didn't know what else to do.

Before he left, Calvin sang to his uncle Yaha. It was a Seminole lullaby his father had sung to him when he was a small boy. Calvin was not a shaman or tribal elder. He hadn't felt right deceiving the nice desk clerk, but since he was here, he decided he should do something for his uncle. Singing the song was all he could think of.

When he finished, he sat still a moment. His uncle Yaha was the only connection he had to his father. Even though Dr. Catal — his grandfather — had caused great harm, he could not blame his uncle for giving a wounded man aid. Uncle Yaha was a healer. Treating the sick and injured was what he had done most of his life.

"It's okay, Uncle Yaha. Rest. I'll think of another way to help Em —" He stopped mid-sentence because Yaha squeezed his hand.

It could have been a reflex. He needed to make sure.

"Uncle? Was that you? Can you hear me?"

Another squeeze.

Calvin was not a shouter, but right now he felt like giving a whoop of joy. Now if only he could figure out a way for Uncle Yaha to tell him where to look for Emmet.

"Uncle, Grandfather has taken Emmet. I need you to tell me where, if you can. I think he has another base in the Everglades. Do you have any idea where it might be? Squeeze my hand if the answer is yes."

Several seconds passed and disappointment seeped into Calvin. Perhaps his uncle could no longer hear him, or perhaps he didn't know the way.

Then Uncle Yaha squeezed his hand. Calvin felt an enormous sense of relief flood over him.

He tried to think of the best way to narrow down the scope of his questions. He would only have a few chances. The Everglades were huge. He could be hidden anywhere. The first time they discovered where Dr. Catalyst was holding Emmet's dad had been mostly sheer luck.

Unlike Emmet, Calvin kept his cell phone in his pocket at all times. He removed it now, using the web browser to pull up a map of the Everglades. He was instantly overwhelmed. There were so many places. The swamp was so vast that it felt like an impossible task. Maybe the best way to start was with a general direction.

"Uncle Yaha, is Grandfather in the north?"

His uncle's hand did not move.

"Is he in the south?" Nothing.

"Is he in the west?" There was a squeeze. Strong and firm. *West!*

"Does Grandfather have Emmet somewhere in the western part of the park?"

Nothing. Uncle Yaha's hand did not move.

"But you said . . ." Calvin was confused. "He's somewhere in the west?"

His uncle squeezed his hand, only this time his grip was stronger, and to Calvin's amazement Yaha pulled him closer. His breathing was heavy and labored.

Calvin watched as he struggled to move his lips. Then he whispered, but Calvin couldn't hear at first. Yaha pulled him forward.

"La . . . ke," Yaha whispered. It sounded like *lakay*.

"One of the Keys? Is he on one of the Keys, Uncle Yaha, in the gulf?" He waited for Yaha to squeeze his hand. He didn't. Calvin had it wrong.

He was just about to ask him another question when a nurse came in. She was carrying a clipboard and had a pair of reading glasses perched on the end of her nose. "Young man, I'm afraid you're going to have to leave. This man needs rest."

"But . . ." Calvin protested.

"No buts, you need to leave now."

Calvin's automatic respect for authority kicked in. With a sad look back at his uncle, he shuffled his way out the door and back to the waiting room. The lady was still sitting at the desk. She smiled at him.

"Can you tell me if my mom is out of surgery yet?" he asked her. "Her last name is Geaux." He spelled it for her and she punched some keys on the keyboard.

"She's being moved to her room." She gave him instructions on how to find it.

Calvin left the waiting room and took the elevator down to her floor, then located the room easily. There was a policeman outside her door. Calvin knew him from the task force, a man named Berman.

"How you holding up, kiddo?" he asked.

"Okay, I guess."

"I heard about what you did with that animal. That was quick thinking."

"Thanks," he said. "Officer Berman, is it okay if I go in and see my mom?"

"Sure, sport. Go right ahead."

Calvin walked in to find his mom lying on the bed. Her head was tilted up and her eyes were closed. There was a scary-looking metal thing encircling her arm where the creature had bitten it. It was held suspended in the air by a bunch of cables and pulleys.

Calvin quietly approached her bedside.

"Mom?" he whispered.

Slowly her eyes fluttered open. A weak smile was all she could manage.

"Hey, buddy," she croaked.

"Mom," he said, trying to keep the tears out of his eyes. "Mom, this is all my fault."

"No, no. Shh," she said. "This is *not* your fault. Don't ever say that."

"But . . ."

"Hush now," she said gently. "You need to stop." She groaned. "Honey, listen. It's going to be okay, but I'm in a lot of pain. I need sleep. What time is it?"

Calvin looked at his phone. It was after two o'clock in the morning.

"You need to get a ride home. Sleep. You can come back tomorrow."

"But —"

"No. Mrs. Clawson will stay with you. Ask Tom or someone on the task force to drive you back home. Sleep in your own bed and come back tomorrow. Okay?"

"Okay, Mom. I will —" Then it hit him. What Yaha had meant. It wasn't one of the Keys. It wasn't *lakay*. It was *lake*. West Lake. Calvin knew right where it was.

"What?" his mom asked. "You will what?"

"I will go home and sleep, and then I'll get a ride back tomorrow. You need to rest, okay?"

Dr. Geaux's eyes were already closed.

As it turned out, Officer Berman's shift was ending. He volunteered to make sure Calvin got home safely. He waited in the drive until Mrs. Clawson made her way from next door, then headed off. There was a squad car parked outside the house. Stuke's dad probably wanted to make sure none of Dr. Catalyst's critters showed up again.

The squad car wasn't a problem. Calvin would be able to elude the watching police officer easily enough.

Calvin waited until Mrs. Clawson went into the guest room. He knew she would never hear him. He gathered his bus pass and his mother's keycard for the entrance to the park headquarters, then he emptied his backpack on the kitchen table.

In the garage he gathered up some tools and other supplies. Then he slipped quietly out of the house, crossing the backyard, and climbed over the fence. Once he reached the creek bank, Calvin began to run.

He had things to do.

22

DR. CATALYST COULDN'T BELIEVE HIS EYES. THE DOYLE brat was right. On the monitor before him were a half dozen news broadcasts from various South Florida stations. All of them were showing his photo. How had this happened?

Then he knew. Yaha had betrayed him. It was the only possible explanation. All his planning. The years of energy and expense. Now everything was in danger of coming to a crashing halt.

The broadcasts summarized his entire life story. He was orphaned at a very young age on the reservation. He was taken in and raised on the rez by relatives, but their means were limited. When the offer came from a young couple to adopt him, it was decided it was in the child's best interest. His adoptive parents were Philip and Marybeth Geaux, young heirs to one of Florida's last great sugar-growing families. They named him Philip Geaux Jr. He grew up surrounded by enormous wealth and privilege. Just as he was leaving for college, his adoptive parents were killed in an automobile accident. They left Philip their vast fortune, but no other family. After college, Philip resurfaced on the Seminole reservation. He married a woman from the tribe and fathered a son with her, but she divorced him when the boy was very young. When he turned his attention to environmental issues, his views grew more and more radical, until even his fellow tribesmen — who were always deeply concerned with the preservation of the Everglades — wanted nothing to do with him.

He was later presumed dead when his airboat was discovered crashed and burned in the Everglades. But his body was never found. In a strange coincidence, his son, Lucas Geaux, who became a well-known hunter and Everglades guide, was also presumed perished in an airboat accident.

And now Philip Geaux Jr. had resurfaced as Dr. Catalyst. Ecoterrorist.

It was all there, his entire story. How could this be? He was no terrorist! He was a visionary! If the Doyle brat hadn't interfered, and Yaha had kept his trap shut, he would be well on his way to saving the Everglades! It was their fault. Why wouldn't anyone listen to him?

Dr. Catalyst stood and stalked through the barn, back and forth, trying to think. He doubted anyone could find this location. All of his many properties had been purchased under layers of false names, dummy corporations, and fake identities. The authorities might know who he really was, but that did not mean they could find him easily.

He strode across the barn to the corner opposite from where he had locked up Emmet Doyle. There stood the pen for his Swamp Cat. The beast was inside the cage and appeared to be mimicking his back-and-forth movement. When he drew near to the enclosure, the beast lunged toward him, its peculiar roar echoing off the walls of the barn. It was a frightening beast. Every part of it, from its mouthful of teeth to the claws on its feet, made it look powerful and deadly. It turned away and prowled toward the corner, melting into the shadows of its cage. It could likely smell Emmet close by. No doubt this was driving the creature mad with hunger.

Dr. Catalyst knew what he must do. He returned to the room he was using as his office and laboratory. He turned on his computer and began sending all of his data — his calculations and formulas, years of experiments — to a secure server at a data farm only he knew about. It would take several hours for all of it to transfer, but by then he would be long gone.

And so would Emmet Doyle.

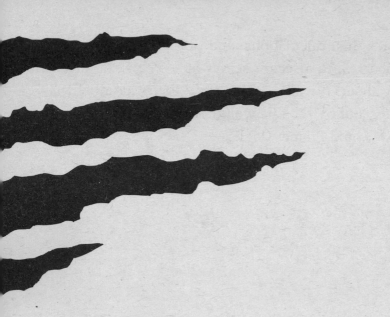

23

CALVIN GOT OFF THE BUS AT THE STOP CLOSEST TO PARK headquarters. He used his mom's keycard to enter the grounds. He remembered how Emmet had first arrived a few months ago, and how they'd encountered the Pterogators. What Calvin had admired about Emmet was his ability to conquer his fear. Calvin was used to the swamp, while Emmet had hated it from the first minute. But despite his wisecracking and obvious discomfort, he always did what needed to be done.

Now it was Calvin's turn. He knew — or at least had a very good idea — where Emmet was. The answer had come to him standing at his mother's bedside. At first he thought his uncle Yaha was telling him that Dr. Catalyst (it was still hard for Calvin to think of the man as his grandfather) was holding Emmet in one of the Keys, the small islands dotting the southern edge of the park. There were literally hundreds of them.

But his uncle had said *west*. Calvin was pretty sure *west* wasn't a direction, it was a specific place: West Lake. It made sense. It was in the center of the park, close to the Taylor Slough. It was not easily accessible, especially by airboat, but there were service roads the park's division had built — trails, really. The lake could be reached for sure by boat and by car. It would give Dr. Catalyst two methods of escape if he was discovered. The land surrounding the lake was marshy, but would suffice to hold an animal like the creature he'd sent after them.

On top of that, Calvin knew there was an abandoned facility on West Lake that would be a perfect hideout. It had once been a veterinary station, where wounded or injured animals were brought and treated by park personnel. Budget cuts had closed the facility years ago. Then someone tried to raise ostriches on it, but that had failed and the land had once again fallen into disrepair. Given the remote location of the lake, it would be an ideal location to stay off the grid.

All he could do was hope he was right. The task force was looking under every rock. But the River of Grass was immense. There were so many places to hide. You could quadruple the size of the task force and they still wouldn't have enough people to look everywhere.

Darting through the gate, Calvin switched on a small flashlight. He headed straight for the trail that led to the docks behind the administration buildings. A few minutes later he boarded the *Dragonfly 1*. His mom had taken the keys away from him, but she didn't know that he kept a second set securely duct-taped inside the access panel.

Calvin quickly went through the checklist to get the boat ready. The fuel tanks were full. The extra container of fuel was also full. He turned the key and powered up the boat. The lights and indicators on his dashboard all showed the boat was operating at full power.

Calvin sat in the pilot seat, thinking. He should call someone — Lieutenant Stukaczowski, or one of the park rangers he knew. He should tell them what he had discovered and where they might be able to find Dr. Catalyst and save Emmet . . . and maybe himself. This was what he *should* do.

But Calvin's greatest strength was also his greatest weakness. His never-ending sense of personal responsibility. Calvin had gone to Yaha to find out about Dr. Catalyst's real identity. Now Dr. Catalyst had been exposed, and Emmet was paying the price for Calvin's actions. He was sure Emmet wasn't hiding in the neighborhood near the hospital, like Stuke's dad had suggested. He felt in his gut that Dr. Catalyst had captured his friend. He couldn't let that pass.

But he wasn't completely without common sense.

Calvin reached inside the small plastic holder on the dash and removed the card inside it. With the always-present felt-tipped pen, he wrote his float plan on the back of the card, along with a note to his mom about where he was going and where he could be found. If he had the chance, he would use the radio and call in the task force. But if Emmet was in danger, well . . . he would have to see.

He stepped out of the boat and onto the dock, then scampered aboard one of the NPS boats, sticking the card inside the holder on its dashboard. Someone would find it in the morning if he wasn't back by then. He climbed back aboard *Dragonfly 1* and fired up the engine. Slowly he backed away from the dock.

Turning the boat, he pointed it straight down the center of the creek leading to the docks. It was now after four A.M. and the night darkness was receding, but still thick. The boat came equipped with a spotlight mounted on the bow. Calvin turned it on and maneuvered it with a toggle switch until it lit up the path over the water in front of him. Calvin knew the swamp well, but one could always collide with a floating log or a big bull gator, which would not be good.

With everything in place and ready, Calvin gave the craft full throttle. The boat literally leapt forward; the fan behind him was spinning at max power. In seconds it was zipping across the water. Like a dragonfly.

Hold on, Emmet. Hold on as long as you can, Calvin thought to himself. *I'm coming.*

24

SINCE THERE WERE NO WINDOWS, EMMET HAD NO idea what time it was until Dr. Catalyst opened the door. He was sitting in the corner, resting but not asleep. After pacing for a while, remembering what Dr. Catalyst had said about being tested in the morning, he thought it would be a good idea to rest. It was a struggle sitting comfortably with his hands behind his back, but he finally managed to relax a little.

Now Dr. Catalyst stood in the doorway, outlined in the dim light of the room. Emmet had no idea what time it was. It must have been close to dawn. That was when the big test was supposed to start.

Part of Emmet was disappointed. He really had expected Calvin to be here by now. Then again, his mother and uncle were in desperate shape at the hospital. Maybe something bad had happened. It made him worry about his dad. Emmet wondered if he was okay.

"Are you ready to surrender?" Emmet asked.

"Stand up," Dr. Catalyst said.

"If you don't mind, I'll sit. I just got comfortable."

"Stand up!" he shouted.

"Okay, okay. Geez, Dr. Crankypants. Out of Cheerios this morning?" There was something different about his face. He looked like someone who was one final straw away from a total breakdown. Emmet pretended to struggle to stand, because his hands were bound behind him. Dr. Catalyst let out a loud sigh of exasperation and bounded across the floor, grabbing Emmet by the arm.

It was the moment Emmet had been waiting for. Emmet let all of his weight sag toward the floor, forcing Dr. Catalyst to lift him off the ground with his good arm. As he did, Emmet kicked his bad arm as hard as he could with his foot. He figured it was still pretty sore from the Pterogator attack. Judging by the man's yelp of pain, it was.

Dr. Catalyst briefly released Emmet, which was all the chance he needed. He ran out the door and into the barn. Emmet slammed the door shut, hoping there was a dead-bolt lock on the other side. No such luck — the door required a key to lock.

He glanced around and spied another door leading outside, then sprinted for it. Of course this one was locked. Emmet turned around and tried fumbling with the lock with his stupid cuffed hands, but he wasn't fast enough. Dr. Catalyst came storming out of the room. Before Emmet could get away he was on him, grabbing him by the shirt collar.

"You little —" Dr. Catalyst muttered through clenched teeth. He dragged Emmet across the floor of the barn. Opposite the room Emmet had been locked in was a steel cage. As they drew nearer to it, a large beast lunged out of the shadows.

It was the Swamp Cat.

It reached through the bars of the cage with its front paw and swiped through the air. It missed taking a chunk out of Emmet by only inches. The Swamp Cat howled again, charging the steel bars so hard Emmet thought it might knock itself out. For some reason, being near Emmet was driving it nearly insane.

Emmet flashed back to that first night it tried to get into their house. How, just for a moment, it had seemed to study him, like it was memorizing his face.

Dr. Catalyst shoved Emmet a few inches closer, and the Swamp Cat lunged again. This time he felt its claws rip through the fabric of his shirt. Dr. Catalyst yanked him back, his vice grip holding him in place.

"Do you see it, Doyle?" he said. "Isn't it magnificent?" Something had changed in him. Emmet was afraid he'd finally truly lost it. And he had no idea what was coming next.

"Oh, yeah," Emmet said. "It's all warm and fuzzy. Here, kitty, kitty, doggy, hyena, whatever you are." The sound of his voice seemed to drive the creature into a renewed frenzy and it lunged again. Emmet was only barely out of reach. For now.

"This is the future. From now on, thanks to me, no ecosystem anywhere will ever need worry about the harm done by an invasive species. I will be able to construct an animal that will destroy the intruders and restore order."

"Really, Grandpa Geaux? Because so far, when it comes to this 'stop the invasive species thing,' you really s —"

Emmet never got to finish, because Dr. Catalyst shoved him toward the cage as the Swamp Cat lunged, and its claws scratched his chest.

"*Ahh!*" he shouted. The Swamp Cat went crazy, throwing its head back and howling with excitement. It licked its paw.

"It's got a taste of you now, boy," Dr. Catalyst said, barely able to keep the glee from his voice. The monster lunged again, but he pulled Emmet back and the paw full of razors sliced through air just inches away from him.

Emmet's chest was on fire. He glanced down to find blood seeping through his shirt. There were four claw marks that had cut right through the cloth as if it weren't there. It hurt. It hurt a lot.

"You're crazy," Emmet said, breathing heavily.

"No. I'm brilliant. You've been wrong about me from the very beginning. Everyone has. I'm a giant and you're a little ant. And now the bug is about to be squashed."

Dr. Catalyst dragged him back to the door leading outside, the one Emmet had been trying to open.

"Wha — what are you doing?" Emmet asked.

"It's time for your test."

"What test? You're crazy. You know that every law enforcement agency in the state is looking for me right now, don't you?"

"They'll never find you in time. Your test will be over and I'll be long gone."

"One more time. *What test* are you talking about? And is it going to be true-or-false or essay questions? I really don't like ess —"

"Enough!" Dr. Catalyst interrupted, throwing open the door. Removing a knife from his pocket, he sliced quickly through the flex-cuffs. Emmet felt a shock of pleasure at having his hands freed, but his relief was short-lived. Dr. Catalyst shoved Emmet through the door, where he landed in a sprawl in the dirt.

"This is an abandoned NPS facility," Dr. Catalyst said. "I repaired the fence and made some improvements. The original fencing was twelve feet tall, so if you get the idea that you can climb out, you should forget it. I ran razor wire along the top. There is only one way out."

"And what would that be?"

"You simply need to survive."

"This would go a lot of faster if you would just say what it is I'm supposed to do."

"Survive."

"Survive *what*?" Emmet shouted. "I don't know what you're talking about!"

"It's simple. This compound has about four hundred acres of surrounding land. You get a ten-minute head start, and then I release my hybrid. If you survive, I'll let you go. If not . . . well . . . I'll be free to continue my work without your interference."

"You're insane," Emmet said again.

"There is a fine line between genius and insanity," Dr. Catalyst said.

"And you've crossed over it and are double-parked in the crazy zone," Emmet said. "You'll never get away with this. They'll find you." Although he was starting to have doubts.

"Really? After all the smart comebacks and wise-cracks, that's all you've got? 'You'll never get away with this'? Frankly, I expected more."

"What are —"

"No more talk," Dr. Catalyst said. "You've got ten minutes. Better start running." He slammed the door in Emmet's face.

Emmet was stunned. Dr. Catalyst was going to let this monstrous creature track him down inside a closed compound, with no way for him to escape. It was crazy. But it didn't seem like Emmet had a lot of choices.

He stood up and he ran.

25

THE GROUND WAS HARD TO RUN ON. IT WAS IN THE middle of a swamp and to call it solid was not exactly accurate. It was so mushy that Emmet's feet sometimes sank up to his ankles. Emmet thought about trying to climb a tree, but there weren't many he saw that would offer much protection from a creature that could probably leap ten feet in the air and climb whatever it wanted. He also suspected Dr. Catalyst hadn't left a bazooka lying around.

The only thing he could think to do was to put as much distance between the barn and himself as he could. Emmet ran along the fence until he came to a corner, then followed it until he came to another corner.

He tried to keep an estimate of how much time he had, but quickly lost track. He just knew it wasn't much.

As Emmet ran, he looked for any kind of weapon to use against the Swamp Cat: a club, a rock, anything that would give him a fighting chance. But he didn't see so much as a stick.

In fact, there were a lot of tree stumps near the fence line — Dr. Catalyst's obvious handiwork. So much for playing fair. There was no way for Emmet to climb a tree and jump over the fence. He probably would have broken both of his ankles on the way down anyway.

Emmet tried scooping out some of the mushy ground at the bottom of the fence, to see if he could tunnel under it, but it seemed to be sunk into the ground a long way. There wouldn't be enough time for him to dig out.

Emmet trotted along the fence, getting more and more desperate as he went. Then, a few yards down from the corner, he saw a cypress branch lying on the ground. It was about five feet long and three inches in diameter, with a slight curve at one end. When he picked it up it felt sturdy. Well, that was something.

Then he remembered the nail.

Emmet pulled it out of his back pocket and stared at it. It was only about four inches long, but it was sharp. He had a stick and a nail. And any second now a wild, hungry beast was going to burst through the brush and eat him. He didn't like his chances. How was he going to make a weapon?

Emmet looked down at his shoes. They were covered in mud and goop, but he realized they had what he needed. As quickly as he could, he removed the shoelace from his right sneaker. He placed the nail alongside the cypress stick, so about three inches of it was sticking out past the end. Emmet then wrapped the shoestring around the stick, so the nail jutted out like the head of a spear. He tied it on as tightly as he could.

If he weren't so desperate, he probably would have laughed at how ridiculous it was. The Swamp Cat would probably bite the stick in half with one chomp. Then one more chomp and Emmet Doyle would go the way of the stick.

He looked out over the grounds. He had to pick a place to make a stand. Emmet backed up against the chain-link fence, right next to one of the support poles. Keeping the fence at his back would give him a better chance of staying on his feet longer. If he could poke the Swamp Cat a few times with his mighty nail spear, maybe it would get discouraged and go eat Dr. Catalyst instead. That would really make his day.

The sun was rising, and the swamp was starting to warm up. Emmet felt hot, sweaty, and tired. Without a bath, he was sure he was giving off all kinds of scents for the animal chasing him. Might as well put up a sign that said MEAL HERE. He wiped his brow with his forearm. It had to have been ten minutes. Where was this thing?

Emmet didn't have to wait long for an answer. From somewhere in front of him, still hidden in the underbrush, came the terrible cry he had grown to fear and loathe.

The Swamp Cat was here.

26

FROM ACROSS THE LAKE, CALVIN STUDIED THE COMPOUND through his binoculars. The boat was hidden behind a hummock of ferns and saw grass. He could see the barn and the fenced-in grounds. The service road leading up to the gate was too muddy to tell if anyone had used it recently. His hopes dimmed. Maybe he was wrong. Perhaps Uncle Yaha had meant something else. He had failed Emmet.

Putting down the binoculars, he studied the map of the Everglades that he carried in the boat. Calvin tried to think of anyplace else that Emmet could be. He was certain he'd understood Yaha correctly, but he had circled the entire lake looking for any sign of Emmet or Dr. Catalyst. There was nothing here.

The *Dragonfly 1* had a quiet electronic motor for trolling. Calvin started it up. On the off chance that Dr. Catalyst was somewhere in the area, he didn't want to alert him. After another turn around West Lake he would head back home. He'd probably get in trouble again, but he would take the punishment. Emmet was counting on him, and Calvin had let his friend down.

Just as he was about to hit the throttle, he heard shouting. Calvin grabbed the binoculars and brought them to bear on the barn. He saw Emmet being shoved out of the door. Dr. Catalyst stood in the doorway. They were yelling back and forth at each other, but Calvin couldn't make out the words. After a few seconds, the door slammed shut. Emmet lay there on the ground a moment as if stunned and then took off running.

He was here. Emmet was here. Uncle Yaha had been right all along.

But why had Emmet been left alone outside? And how could Calvin get his attention without alerting Dr. Catalyst? He still didn't have a clear idea what was going on, but he pushed forward on the throttle and maneuvered the boat the remaining distance from the center of the lake toward the compound. The sun was coming up, but hopefully he would still be hidden well enough by the darkness to keep Dr. Catalyst from discovering him.

A few minutes later the boat nudged up against the

shore and Calvin scrambled out. He tied the bowline to a mangrove root and, with his backpack in hand, headed toward the fence. Standing next to it, he realized it was impossibly tall. There was no way to climb it.

Staring through the chain links, he could no longer spot Emmet. There were too many trees and shrubs in the way. He still had no idea what was happening or what was the best way to help Emmet. Why had Dr. Catalyst shoved him out the door of the barn? Was he letting Emmet go?

His question was answered when a small metal door on the side of the barn slid open and the cat creature immediately slinked through it. Calvin couldn't believe his eyes. Dr. Catalyst was sending the beast after Emmet. Emmet would never stand a chance.

Calvin pulled out his cell phone and hit the emergency button. It would send a distress signal to the task force, and they would send help immediately. But it would take them time to get here. He had to do something.

He slung the backpack off his shoulder and dug inside, removing a pair of bolt cutters. The same bolt cutters he and Emmet used to break into Undersea Land and rescue Apollo not long ago.

He had an idea.

With the bolt cutters, he went to work on the chain-link fence.

Snipping away.

27

AS HUNGRY AND FURIOUS AS THE SWAMP CAT WAS, IT didn't launch itself at Emmet immediately. There must have been something in its predatory brain that forced it to pause to take stock of its prey before it attacked. It stood ten yards away, snarling and howling. Emmet could tell from its crouched posture that an attack was imminent.

Living in Montana and spending time outdoors with his dad had taught Emmet a little bit about wild animals. Montana had grizzlies, mountain lions, and wolves. The big difference between Florida and Montana predators was that the ones in Montana couldn't hide under the water or fly down on you from the sky. Or both. Usually you could see them coming.

One of the things Emmet's dad taught him that might prevent an animal from attacking was to make a lot of noise and try to make yourself appear bigger. Raising your hands over your head and jumping up and down screaming could sometimes scare it away. It was all he had. That and a stick with a nail tied to it.

Emmet yelled with everything in him, raising his arms over his head. His primitive spear was in one hand, and he banged it against the fence, screaming at the top of his lungs.

The Swamp Cat crouched lower to the ground. Its eyes bored into him.

"Get away! Get away! Yah! Yah!" Emmet shouted.

It only bought him a few seconds. The animal leapt forward. Its forelegs were extended and it seemed like every claw on its paws was at least a foot long. Emmet was amazed at how far it could jump. It felt like time slowed down and the creature was floating in the air. One swipe from its paw would likely take his head off.

Emmet almost didn't react in time. Right when it was about two feet away, Emmet dropped to the ground and stabbed up with the spear. The point of the nail struck the Swamp Cat in the shoulder, and it crashed face-first into the fence. It howled in pain and confusion. Emmet tumbled out of the way.

He came to his feet and held the spear out in front of him at the ready. The animal slid down the fence and rolled back onto its feet, shaking its head. There was a small trickle of blood on its shoulder. The sight of it made Emmet feel just a tiny bit better.

"Come on, you giant bag of teeth!" he shouted. "If I'm going down, I'm going down swinging. Or stabbing. Whatever!"

The creature growled and shook its head one more time, stalking toward him. Emmet decided he needed to show the Swamp Cat he would not be an easy meal. He backed up a few steps, then gave a loud war cry and rushed forward, brandishing the spear.

"Hah! Hah!" Emmet shouted, stabbing at the creature. It batted at the stick, as if they were playing some deadly game.

Emmet tried to find an opening, but with each lunge of the spear the beast darted out of the way.

As he was backing up to prepare for another lunge, Emmet tripped over something, landing flat on his back and losing the spear. The animal was on him in an instant, pinning him to the ground with its paws on his shoulders. One of its claws pierced his flesh, and he cried out in agony.

All Emmet could think to do was put his hands around the Swamp Cat's throat, trying desperately to cut off its air supply. But the massive, muscular creature was far too strong. It was taking every ounce of his strength to keep the jaws from reaching his throat. In desperation, Emmet let go with one hand and scooped up a handful of muddy soil, shoving it into the beast's eyes.

Temporarily blinded, it jumped backward, shaking its head and trying to clear its vision. Emmet's shoulder was screaming in pain, but he didn't waste any time, jumping to his feet and clutching the spear with his good arm. He took off running.

Emmet had no illusions that he could outrun the creature. Besides, he was wounded and was feeling a little light-headed. Despite that, Emmet sprinted as fast as he could along the fence. Instinct told him to stay by the fence. It gave the creature one less direction to attack him from. There was a very loud, very angry growl coming from somewhere to his rear.

The bushes and grasses behind him rustled as the creature plowed its way through them. It growled again. It was gaining. It had to be almost upon him. There was nothing else to do but face it.

Emmet whirled around and held the spear out in front of him. The Swamp Cat was closing fast. He was about to shut his eyes and plow ahead with his weapon when the fence flew forward all on its own. The beast crashed into it with a surprised yelp.

Somehow Calvin was there, standing ankle-deep in muck, and he was pushing a rectangular section of the fencing back toward the fence, trapping the Swamp Cat within.

"Emmet!" he shouted "Help me!"

Emmet couldn't believe what he was seeing. Calvin was there. Somehow he'd cut out a big rectangular section of the fence and he was struggling to push it around the thrashing Swamp Cat.

"Emmet!" Calvin shouted, and Emmet jumped. The Swamp Cat was growling and snarling but it was tangled up in the fence, temporarily caged. "Hurry!"

He joined Calvin and together they kept pushing until the fence had folded all the way back on itself with the beast trapped inside. They dug into the ground with their feet and shoved.

"What did you do?" Emmet shouted.

"Push now. Talk later," Calvin grunted. The Swamp Cat was incredibly strong. It was flopping all around, snarling and clawing, but with the fence folded back on it, it was like a horse in a stall. It couldn't go anywhere.

Calvin pulled a bungee cord from around his shoulder and tied the cut piece of fencing to one of the support poles. The Swamp Cat was trapped as long as the cord held.

"First I was just trying to cut an opening so I could get inside," Calvin huffed. "Then I saw you running along the fence and I figured you were looking for a way to climb it. When this thing came out of the barn, I knew you were in trouble. So I cut out a section, hoping we could trap it. I'm just glad you stayed by the fence."

Emmet couldn't believe it. His mind was racing, making it hard to think. They were safe. Also, his shoulder really hurt.

"Come on, we've got to go," Calvin said. "This trap won't hold for long. I've got the boat right over —"

"You're not going anywhere, *grandson*," said a voice from behind them.

Emmet and Calvin turned around, and there stood Dr. Catalyst.

And he had a gun.

28

"**S**O YOU LIED?" EMMET SAID.

Emmet had to admit, even though Dr. Catalyst had given his hair a really bad dye job, he looked a lot like Calvin's dad. At least from the picture Emmet had seen. It must have shaken him up.

"You lied!" Emmet repeated. "You said if I survived, you'd let me go."

Dr. Catalyst shrugged. "So I lied. But I'm glad you're here, Calvin. You have disgraced our family, helping these people who have been systematically destroying your ancestral homeland. What a disappointment you are."

Emmet looked at Calvin. Most of the time his expression rarely changed. A lifted eyebrow or a shrug was it when it came to showing his emotions. But now Emmet saw something on his friend's face that he didn't think he'd ever seen before. Calvin was angry.

"What did you say?" Calvin asked, his voice barely more than a whisper.

"I said your behavior has disgraced your family name," Dr. Catalyst said.

"I'm not the one who lost his way!" Calvin shouted. "I'm not the one who polluted the River of Grass with your abominations of nature! Don't try to push your failures off on me! If your son were alive to see what you've become, *he* would hang his head in shame. Then he would turn you in himself!"

Wow. Go Calvin. Emmet was going to pipe up, but it sounded like a family matter. Best to let them work out their issues.

"Don't you mention my son," Dr. Catalyst hissed.

"Why? Because I spoke the truth? My father loved the Glades. All you've done is try to destroy the people who are working to save it. What is it, Grandfather? Do you feel guilty because you were taken from the reservation and were raised in wealth and privilege? Upset that when you returned to the Seminole Nation no one there would accept you? You didn't fit in, so you faked your death? You say you fooled with Mother Nature to *save* the Everglades? You're destroying them!"

Behind Emmet, the Swamp Cat was still struggling

and thrashing. The fence was holding for now, but he wasn't sure how much longer it would cage the cat.

"Destroying it? I'm single-handedly saving it! And I'll continue to save it. I don't care if you're my grandson or not. You've interfered long enough. I'm through talking."

Dr. Catalyst raised the gun, pointing it in their direction. Neither of them had a chance to even say anything. This was it.

Rifle shots exploded in the ground in front of Dr. Catalyst. A helicopter burst over the horizon, and then another and another.

"Drop the weapon!" a voice shouted through a loudspeaker.

Emmet heard a *poof* sound from behind them, and the Swamp Cat snarled. He turned to see a tranquilizer dart sticking out of its side. The creature laughed — the strange, manic cackle of a hyena — for a few seconds before collapsing to the ground. *Nighty night,* Emmet thought deliriously.

"Drop the weapon and get down on your knees! Last warning!" Emmet now recognized the voice as Stuke's dad. Dr. Catalyst tossed the pistol aside and dropped to his knees. Two helicopters landed nearby. An FBI tactical team burst out of them and had him in handcuffs in seconds.

Emmet couldn't remember the last time he was so happy. Two men got out of one of the choppers, Lieutenant Stukaczowski and another man, who had shaggy hair and was limping a little bit. His face was covered with scratches and what looked like bite marks.

"You boys okay?" asked Lieutenant Stukaczowski.

Emmet didn't answer because he was looking at the other guy.

"Dr. Newton?" he said. It *was* him. The Newt.

He pulled a wallet out of his back pocket and held it up. Out flashed a bright, shiny badge.

"Actually, it's Special Agent Newton of Interpol," he said.

"Agent who of what?" Emmet said.

Newton laughed.

"You're too much, Emmet," he said. "I'm an undercover Interpol agent. Interpol is an international law enforcement agency that deals in cases like this, involving the international import and export of exotic animals. When you started accusing me of being Dr. Catalyst, I thought you were going to blow up years of work. I've been after this nut job for a long time. But I guess if I'm honest, without you I never would have caught him."

"We thought you died," Calvin said.

"I almost did. A couple of times," he said.

"You've got a lot of explaining to do," Emmet said. For some reason he couldn't pin down, he still didn't quite trust him. But he did look like he'd recently been put through a meat grinder.

Newton laughed again. "I know. But right now we're going to get you guys home. Emmet, you need to get that shoulder treated. One of these choppers will take you to Miami to your parents. I've got to stay with my team and gather evidence. But I promise we'll talk, okay?"

Emmet looked at Calvin. You wouldn't know it unless you knew him like Emmet did, but he was as confused as anyone.

He shrugged.

Epilogue

EMMET'S DAD WAS FINALLY UP AND AROUND. A COUPLE of more days in the hospital and he would be able to come home. They were both in Dr. Geaux's room with Calvin. They'd even brought along Apollo, telling the nurses he was Emmet's therapy dog. Right now his "therapy" was lying on Dr. Geaux's bed, getting a belly rub from her one good hand. She was on a lot of pain-killers, but not enough to miss out on a scolding.

"I can't believe you two!" she said. "What does it take to get through to you? What you did was dangerous and . . . and . . . you're both just lucky that I can't get out of bed."

"Sorry, Dr. Geaux," Emmet said. "But to be fair, Dr.

Catalyst captured me. It was Calvin who took off again and disobeyed orders."

"Dude!" Calvin said. Emmet gave him a big grin, to which Calvin narrowed his eyes in response.

"What matters is that you're both safe," Emmet's dad said. "And Dr. Catalyst is in custody. We don't have to worry about him anymore."

There was a part of Emmet that wondered about that. Dr. Catalyst was slippery and had a lot of resources. Was this really the end of him?

"Yeah, I suppose," Emmet said. He turned to Calvin. "But, hey, they said your uncle Yaha is in stable condition now. It was pretty brave of him to take on the Swamp Cat like that. I guess we all owe him our lives."

"I guess we do," Dr. Geaux said.

"I have to say, this is one weird story. I mean, your grandfather? After all these years?"

"Emmet," Calvin said. "I want you to know . . . I'm sorry I didn't speak up sooner. If —"

Emmet held up his hand. "Calvin, it's okay. I get it. And you saved my life. A couple of times now. We're even."

"But —" Calvin started.

"You've talked more in the last twenty-four hours than you have since I've known you," Emmet said. "I understand why you did what you did. We're cool. Besides, there are more interesting things to discuss, like, say, Dr. Newton is an Interpol agent? The Newt?

Everybody thought he died in the swamp. I wonder how he made it out?"

Calvin, realizing he was out of trouble with Emmet, visibly relaxed. And then he shrugged.

"See," Emmet said. "The old Calvin is back."

"So what's next?" Dr. Geaux asked.

"Peace and quiet, I hope," said Emmet. "And fewer teeth. Fewer teeth would be really good."

Emmet's dad laughed.

"We'll do our best to limit your exposure to nature for a while," he said.

"I don't think that's possible in Florida, Dad. Everywhere you go there's something with teeth. Alligators in your swimming pool, snakes in the trees. It's impossible to go anyplace without a pretty good chance of something biting you."

Dr. Geaux had a serious, almost sad expression on her face now.

"Benton, now that the crisis is over, what will you do?" she asked. "Will you go back to Montana?"

Dr. Doyle was quiet a moment.

"I don't know, Rosalita," he said. "There are still some Pterogators in the park. I think I need to help your team make sure they're all rounded up before they cause more problems. But I need to discuss it with Emmet. We haven't had a chance yet."

He looked at Emmet.

"Emmet, what do you think? How do you feel about staying in Florida, at least for a while?"

Emmet didn't answer right away. In his mind's eye he could see the snow-capped peaks of Montana. The roaring rivers and the soaring eagles. Emmet saw himself snowboarding and hiking the trails with his dad. Montana was where he'd lived after his mother died, where he'd mourned her. He'd found a kind of peace there. It was a peace that had been quickly shattered when they arrived in Florida City. He missed it.

But then he looked around the room at Dr. Geaux and Calvin. And even at Apollo, who was happy right where he was. Emmet realized in all the craziness of the past few months that he hadn't had much time to think about his mom. Maybe now, with life a bit calmer, he and his dad could focus on rebuilding their family. Or building a new one.

"I don't know, Dad. I guess it would be all right to stay for a while," Emmet said. All four of them smiled. "Don't go acting all relieved yet," he said. "You haven't heard my one condition."

"What's that?" his dad asked.

"I am *never*, under any circumstances, going back in that swamp."

Everyone laughed, and Emmet's dad clapped him on the shoulder.

"That's a deal."

FROM DR. CATALYST'S FILES

"Swamp Cat"

Sharp sense of smell!

Hyena and panther — not so different

Trained to HUNT
EMMET DOYLE

My finest
creation EVER?

CHAPTER 1
THE DARKEST PLACE

The house, when they finally found it, was like nothing Morton had ever seen in the city. Tucked away at the end of a winding gravel driveway and veiled in curtains of tangled ivy, it loomed behind a dense row of trees like an ancient lost monument.

"Here we are," Dad announced cheerily as they pulled up to the end of the driveway. "Eighty-eight Hemlock Hill. Our new home."

Morton felt a jolt of excitement wash away the tensions of the long journey. Could it be true? Could this immense old house really be their new home? He clambered forward from the backseat to get a better view. To Morton it looked almost like a small castle. There was a tall round turret at the front and long wide porches wrapping around the sides. It had countless windows of all shapes and sizes, and there were at least two large upstairs balconies. Morton began to get so excited he felt he might burst. It had to be three times bigger than their old house.

"You've got to be kidding me!" a morose voice intoned

from beside Morton. It was Melissa, his sixteen-year-old sister. "That's not a house, it's a ruin."

"It does look kind of run-down," agreed James, Morton's thirteen-year-old brother, who was also squashed uncomfortably in the backseat.

"I hate it!" Melissa added, as if declaring a guilty verdict at a trial.

Morton turned to look at them in bewilderment. "What are you talking about? It's perfect!" he exclaimed.

"Well, of course you'd like it. You're a freak," Melissa scoffed.

"What's that supposed to mean?"

"It's ghastly, creepy, and almost certainly haunted. In fact, it's like something right out of that horrid comic you read all the time."

Morton looked up at the house again. It was true; it did look a little neglected. Some of the windows were cracked, shingles were missing, and the paint was peeling here and there, giving way to green mildew, but surely that was all part of the charm.

"I told you it was a stupid idea to buy a house without seeing it," Melissa said with a scowl.

Dad ignored Melissa's comment and climbed stiffly out of the car to gaze up at the old building. Morton wriggled over to the front seat and bounded out after him. Melissa and James followed suit, throwing the back doors open wide and stepping out onto the gravel driveway.

"I suppose it is a little worse than it looked in the picture," Dad admitted, in his clipped British accent. "But it's not that bad. Anyway, it wouldn't be any fun if we didn't get to fix it up and make it our own, would it?"

"No offense, Dad," James said, stretching his arms and legs, "but you're not exactly the world's best handyman."

Morton had to agree with James on this point. Whenever Dad tried to do anything around the house he inevitably bungled it, and it had always been Mum who'd swooped in with a big smile to save the day. But now . . .

"Don't they have normal houses in this freak show of a town?" Melissa pouted.

"But it's a cool house," Morton said, feeling irritated by Melissa's barrage of pessimism. "And what's wrong with the town?"

"Didn't you see that sign as we drove in?" Melissa went on. "It said, 'Welcome to Dimvale, the Darkest Town in the Civilized World.' What's that all about?"

Dad began rubbing his temples. "I'm quite sure I've explained the situation to you at least a dozen times," he said, trying to sound patient. "Astronomers need absolute darkness to get good results. Dimvale is one of the few places left in North America that has bylaws controlling light pollution, which is why I jumped at the chance to work at the Dimvale Observatory."

" 'Bylaws controlling light pollution'? What does that even mean?" Melissa asked suspiciously.

"It means no neon signs, no office buildings spilling light into the sky, no unnecessary street lights. . . ."

"No street lights! Are you sure this place actually is civilized?"

"I assure you it has everything you need. It has a cinema, a library, lots of restaurants. It even has a school."

"Oh, a school! So glad you didn't overlook that little detail. I'll bet they don't have any good shoe stores," Melissa said, crossing her arms and sinking into a big sulk.

"Melissa, it's going to be just fine," Dad said soothingly. "Come on, let's explore inside."

After being stuck in the car for five hours, this, at least, was something everyone was happy to do. They followed Dad along the path to the sagging porch at the back of the house. Dad produced an old key from under the doormat and clicked the lock open with a satisfied smile.

Morton thought the inside was even better than the outside. True, there was a lot of cracked plaster, and several of the rooms had ugly wallpaper, but the grand, high ceilings and beautifully preserved original woodwork more than made up for that. Everything smelled of furniture wax and mothballs, and Morton felt instantly at home, which was odd because the house couldn't have been more different from their clean, sterile, modern place in the city. Morton decided this had something to do with the fact that the movers had already delivered all of their furniture and boxes, which had been neatly arranged in the appropriate rooms.

Dad immediately led them on a brief tour, and both James's and Melissa's moods seemed to pick up when they saw their new spacious bedrooms. James was particularly pleased because he and Morton had always had to share a room up until now.

"You've got to admit, it's pretty cool," Morton said to James as they trooped through the house.

"I guess it will be nice not to have to listen to you snoring all night," James said, ruffling Morton's wavy hair.

"I don't snore," Morton protested, and then James laughed for the first time since Morton could remember.

"Just kidding," James said.

"And last but not least," Dad was saying, "this is Morton's room."

The three kids followed Dad to the very end of the narrow upstairs landing into a large bedroom at the back.

"Whoa! This is awesome!" Morton said, pushing past the others to get a good look. The room was at least twice the size of the one he used to share with James, with two large windows and a small door leading to one of the balconies he'd seen from outside. Not only did he get his own balcony but now he'd also have more than enough room for his large collection of comics and toys. Morton threw his arms around Dad's waist and squeezed him tight. "Thanks, Dad. I love it."

Dad looked over at James and Melissa. "You see," he said, raising his eyebrows. "Not so bad, eh?"

James nodded appreciatively while Melissa kind of

shrugged and chewed her nails, which was as close as she'd come to agreeing with Dad.

"Now," Dad went on, "how about you lot start unpacking the small stuff, and I'll see about fixing us some lunch." And he paced off down the stairs, leaving the three kids alone.

Melissa glared at James and Morton. "Living in this place is going to be a nightmare. You know that, right?"

"I dunno," James said. "My nightmares don't usually have spacious bedrooms with balconies overlooking the flower garden."

Melissa sneered. "There you go again."

"What?" James said.

"Trying to make jokes about everything."

"I'm being serious," James said, with a teasing smile. "I've never had a nightmare about flower gardens."

Morton braced himself for this teasing exchange to explode into the now familiar all-out fight, but to his relief Melissa bit her tongue and stomped off down the hallway to her new bedroom.

James shrugged. "It *may* actually be a nightmare with her around," he said.

Morton didn't reply. Things had been so tense between James and Melissa recently that it was pretty much unbearable any time they were in the same room together. James couldn't seem to resist winding Melissa up, and Melissa had become more petulant and moody than ever.

"What's up?" James asked, as if sensing Morton's mood.

Morton sighed. "I don't know," he said. "It's just, why do you two always have to fight? It's not fun anymore."

James reflected on this for a moment and then snapped his fingers. "You know what *is* fun?" he said. "Attic hunting. There's sure to be one in this old house."

Morton hadn't even thought of that. He'd seen the large peaked roof from the outside, but Dad hadn't mentioned anything about an attic on the tour. That would be fun, he thought, and moments later he and James were racing around the upstairs, looking in all the corners and cubbies. They soon found a narrow, dusty staircase hidden behind what appeared to be a door to a small closet.

"Whoa!" James said. "Jackpot."

Morton peered up. The stairs vanished into complete blackness. James flipped a tarnished old brass light switch mounted just inside the door with no result.

"Looks like the bulb's gone. Maybe we should wait until . . ."

But Morton wasn't about to wait. All his life he'd wanted to live in a house with a big old attic. He bounded up the bare wooden steps, his eyes rapidly adjusting to the dim light, until he arrived on a narrow landing at the top.

James hesitated below.

"Come on," Morton called. "Your eyes get used to it pretty quick."

"Aren't you afraid of the dark?" James said, timidly following him up the stairs. "Most kids your age won't even go to bed without a night-light, never mind dash up into a strange attic."

"You can't be afraid of something that's not there," Morton said matter-of-factly.

James arrived on the landing and stood next to him. There was a second door, much older than the first, with a large ragged hole in the woodwork, and Morton could see dim shapes in the attic beyond.

"But darkness is there," James said. "I can see it."

Morton shook his head. "Darkness is the absence of light. It's not actually anything, and you can't be afraid of nothing."

"I can," James said, looking through the hole in the door. "In fact, I'm very good at it."

"I learned a trick from *Scare Scape* issue 275," Morton said. "The story about the boy lost in an abandoned mine shaft. He had to find his way out in the complete dark and he kept telling himself that darkness was nothing, but it still made him afraid, so he started shouting, 'I *am* afraid of nothing, I *am* afraid of nothing.' And then he realized that was the same as saying he wasn't afraid, so then he wasn't afraid, get it?"

James scratched his head. "You know, that almost makes sense. Not quite, but almost."

"So now you don't have to be afraid of the dark either," Morton said, and without pausing he pushed the broken door open and stepped into the gloom beyond.

The attic couldn't have been more perfect. It had tall

sloped ceilings, rough-sawn rafters covered in cobwebs, and an uneven planked floor scattered with old discarded objects. There were moth-eaten suitcases, a moldering baby carriage, and several old wooden trunks. Strangely, like the rest of the house, the attic had an air of familiarity to it. Yet this time Morton realized exactly why.

"Hey, this reminds me of another story in *Scare Scape*," Morton said excitedly. "The one where the lawyer gets an infestation of Flesh-Eating Cockroaches in his attic. You must remember that one?"

James stepped timidly into the attic and gave a thin smile. "Ever think you might be getting too old for that comic, Morton?"

Morton sighed, feeling a pang of disappointment. *Scare Scape* had once been James's favorite comic too, but over the last few years his interest had waned completely. Some of Morton's fondest memories were of the times they'd stayed up late reading and talking and making up their own creepy stories. In fact, it had been James who first showed him the comic, and it had been James who bought Morton his first mail-order monster, starting off his prized collection of *Scare Scape* toys.

James didn't seem to notice Morton's disappointment and turned to look at the tiny, cracked windows that were casting hazy shafts of light across the room. "How do you suppose they all got broken?" he asked.

Morton shrugged. "Kids throwing stones?"

James shook his head. "We're too high up for that."

Morton looked again at the disheveled attic. A standing lamp had fallen and smashed, several boxes were on their sides, and sawdust had spilled from a large wooden crate in the corner. This really was like something from one of the creepy stories in *Scare Scape*.

"You think somebody might have been trapped in here?" Morton said, in an excited whisper.

"Uh, maybe we should go," James said, his mood suddenly shifting. But before either of them had time to turn, a sudden scratching noise made them freeze on the spot. Something was moving behind one of the old trunks. Morton and James stared at each other.

"Mice?" James asked hopefully.

"Uh-uh," Morton said. "Too big for a mouse. Could be a Visible Fang."

"A what?"

"Visible Fang. You know, the creature with a transparent body, likes to hide in attics and basements."

James looked around nervously. "You do know those creatures in your comic aren't real, right?"

Morton grinned. This was starting to be fun.

The scratching noise came again, and this time it seemed to be coming from inside the trunk, not behind it.

"Well, it's definitely too big for a mouse," Morton repeated firmly. "So I don't know what else it could be."

James swallowed hard. "Why would Visible Fangs be in an attic anyway?"

"Don't you remember? They like to live near people. They creep down into their houses at night and hypnotize them."

"Oh, yeah, what was all that about? They'd hypnotize you and then steal stuff?"

"No, you're getting them confused with Swag Sprites," Morton replied. "The Visible Fang paralyzes you with hypnosis so it can eat your heart out while you're asleep."

"Oh, right," James said, a distinct tremor in his voice. "Now I remember."

"Didn't they used to be your favorite?" Morton asked.

"No. That was the Toxic Vapor Worms. They were the coolest."

"Hey, you never read the issue where the Visible Fangs and the Toxic Vapor Worms teamed up, did you?"

"I don't think so."

"It's awesome. Do you want me to lend it to you sometime?" Morton asked, a hopeful note in his voice.

James opened his mouth to respond but the scratching noise came again, and this time there was no doubt that it was coming from inside the old trunk.

"It can't really be a Visible Fang, can it?" James whispered, looking genuinely afraid now.

"Only one way to find out," Morton said, and without even thinking about it he stepped swiftly forward and threw the lid open. There was a sudden screech and the fierce rattle of claws scratching on wood. Morton heard

James let out a shriek and saw him fall to the floor just as a fast-moving gray blur flew out of the trunk, bounded onto James's leg, and then rushed to one of the tiny windows. Morton spun quickly around to see the creature's body silhouetted in the cracked glass. A small head with a curved body and a large fluffy tail. It was a fat gray squirrel. It chirped angrily at them before disappearing through the hole in the broken window.

"It was just a squirrel," Morton said, surprised to feel his heart pounding against his ribs.

James lay motionless on his back, his face as white as chalk. For a moment Morton couldn't interpret James's expression, then quite unexpectedly he began to laugh. Morton felt a wave of relief and started laughing too, and before he knew it, they were both rolling around on the dusty wooden floorboards, practically suffocating with laughter.

Just like the old days, Morton thought, and for the first time in months he dared to hope that things were going to get back to normal.

James finally stopped laughing and stood up. "Come on, Squirto," he said, offering his hand to Morton. "We'd better go help unpack or Dad will give us one of his long speeches about pulling our weight."

Morton grabbed on to James's hand and got to his feet.

"Hey, I know which box that Toxic Vapor Worm and Visible Fang issue is in. Do you want me to get it for you?" Morton asked as he followed James down the stairs.

"Sure," James said, "but I should get started unpacking."

The two of them stepped back out onto the wide landing.

"I'll bring it to you," Morton said eagerly.

"Okay, then, but don't get lost in this big creepy house of ours," James said with a wry smile. "And look out for Kamikaze Cobras."

Morton chuckled again and sprinted to his new room at the end of the hallway. Since Morton had insisted on packing his moving boxes himself, he knew exactly what he was looking for. He quickly found the box marked SCARE SCAPE, ISSUES 200 TO 400 and ripped the tape from its lid. The familiar, comforting smell of old musty paper filled his nostrils. He pulled issue 237 from the box and was about to run from the room when he noticed something odd about the front cover. It had a shadowy illustration of a girl who looked exactly like Melissa. She was tall and skinny, with jet-black hair and dark brown, almost black, eyes. The girl was screaming, terrified of a giant centipede-like creature. Funny, Morton thought, he must have seen this cover a hundred times but never noticed the resemblance before now.

He put the lid back on the box and rushed down the hall to James's room. The door was closed, but he burst in without knocking.

"Hey, I found that issue, and it's the weirdest thing — the girl on the cover looks just like Melissa. . . ."

Morton stopped short. James was huddled in a corner over an open moving box, with his hands covering his face.

"James?" Morton asked softly.

After what seemed like too long a pause James turned around, wiping his face with his sleeve. "Oh, wow!" he said, putting on a crooked smile. "The dust in this place is out of control. Just look at me, allergies totally gone berserk!"

James's eyes were bright pink and his cheeks were wet.

"Here's that issue we talked about," Morton said, wishing suddenly that he'd knocked first.

"Oh, yeah, thanks," James said, holding the same crooked smile, and without even looking at the comic, he took it from Morton's hand and placed it on his small desk. "I'll read it later."

Morton nodded and began to shuffle awkwardly out of the room. "Yeah, I better go, uh, unpack," he said, and a moment later he was standing in the hallway with his back to the wall as an odd choking feeling seemed to envelop him.

No, not like the old days, he thought. It had been stupid of him to even think that. It would never be like the old days again.

VISIBLE FANG

The defining characteristic of this rare creature is its reclusive nature. It avoids being seen by taking advantage of its translucent body and confining itself to shadowy places. Despite its diamond-hard fang, from which it gets its name, it has never been known to attack conscious prey, instead first using some as yet unverified hypnotic technique to place its victims in a trance. Though it will eat anything, it is believed that it prefers dense muscular organs, particularly the heart.

It is also said that the Fang avoids crowds, seeking out houses where people live in solitude. This is almost certainly true, though some debate continues about why the Fang adopts this habit. Some claim it is a purely defensive strategy, while others suggest that the hypnotic powers of the Fang are more effective on vulnerable and lonely souls.

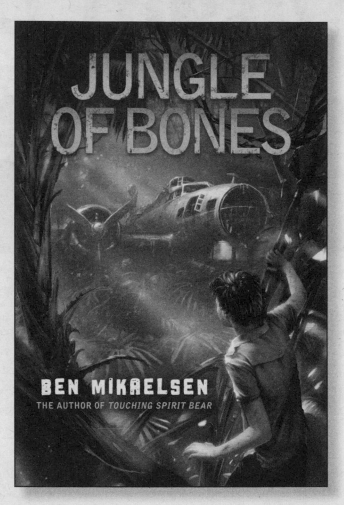